A JOURNEY OF FAITH

THREE COWBOYS FOR THREE SISTERS, BOOK ONE

VICTORIA WINTERS

Published by Blushing Books
An Imprint of
ABCD Graphics and Design, Inc.
A Virginia Corporation
977 Seminole Trail #233
Charlottesville, VA 22901

Victoria Winters
A Journey of Faith

EBook ISBN: 978-1-61258-999-2
Print ISBN: 978-1-64563-038-8
v1

Cover Art by ABCD Graphics & Design

CHAPTER 1

aith Cummings cracked open the window and set the pie she had just baked on the sill to cool. She poured herself a cup of tea and sat, watching the curtains at the open window fluttering in the breeze. The entire house felt different, as if a dark cloud had lifted. Even the air felt lighter. Her father had recently passed. She could hardly believe that he was no longer upstairs in his room. He had not been much company at the end, but at least he'd been there, someone for her to focus on and care for. She shook her head to clear her thoughts then moved the pie inside and shut the window. While it had been nice to air out the room, it was not yet spring in Boston and too cold to leave the window open for long. She hugged herself and shivered. Change was in the air; she could feel it.

Faith did not much care for change. She had been well named, faithfully nursing her father without complaint throughout his long decline. She was content to stay at home, running the

1

household while her younger, more adventurous sisters, Hope and Charity, went out into the world making social calls, serving on committees and doing volunteer work. Why, Hope even had a job of sorts, helping set print at the newspaper, and Charity appeared in productions at the local community playhouse. She admired her sisters but had no desire to be like them.

She went to the fireplace and bent to stoke the fire. Her sisters would be home soon, and she wanted the house to be warm and welcoming, the very house that soon would no longer be theirs. Without Father's pension, it would have to be sold; the girls could not afford the mortgage on their own.

Faith could hardly bear to dwell on the future. What was she going to do now? At twenty-eight, she was certain that marriage and motherhood had passed her by. Why, she had never even had a serious suitor. She didn't want to become a governess and work for strangers; children made her nervous. She supposed she could take in laundry or work as a cook, but she preferred to bake. Everyone said her pies were heavenly; perhaps she could sell them to the restaurants in town. Boston was a big city, and there could be a demand, but she could only produce half a dozen or so pies a day. It would barely provide pin money, certainly not enough to live respectably on. She blew on the flame that was just starting to burn brightly then stood and studied her reflection in the looking glass hanging over the mantel. She was a slender woman, neat and tidy in a dark grey dress with an apron pinned to the front. Faith really did not know why she had never had a caller. She had grown up thinking she was plain with her blue-grey eyes and light brown curls, but Hope said she had the kind of beauty that grew on a person. Charity had agreed and said she drew people in with her smile. Faith was just so painfully shy that she didn't often gift strangers with her smile.

Just then, she heard someone at the front door, stomping the snow off their boots. Hope must be home. Sure enough, her younger sister opened the door and strode into the house. Strode was a good word for how she walked. At the age of twenty-four, Hope was a large woman with long, thick, chestnut-colored hair who acted more like a man than a young lady. Faith greeted her sister and went to pour her a cup of tea. Hope was also well named. She had an adventurous spirit and was filled with hopes and dreams for the future.

"I'm home," Hope announced unnecessarily. "I've just been to the county assessor's office and then ran an advertisement in the newspaper for the house. They say there's a big demand, and it should sell shortly. And guess what?"

Faith shook her head as she handed the tea to Hope. She could not even begin to guess what had her sister so excited.

"There was a flyer hanging on a post outside the assessor's office. It said that there is land up for grabbing, out west! We could homestead on a plot of land, do some improvements, and then in a couple of years, it would be ours. Why, we could work it ourselves, build our own home. Think of it, Faith, wouldn't that be wonderful?"

Faith was aghast. "We can't just up and move; they don't call it the wild west for nothing. Why, there are cowboys and Indians and outlaws. People carry guns. It's downright uncivilized. And besides, what would we do with all our belongings?" Faith asked.

Hope tapped her foot impatiently as she looked down at her timid older sister.

"What? It's better to sit here in this house, staring out the window? Why, there's a whole world out there, Faith! It's ours for the taking."

"Well, we certainly can't leave our little sister alone in Boston," Faith stated with finality, hopefully bringing an end to the discussion. She wondered what it would be like to have such a fearless and adventurous spirit. She, herself, had never suffered from the wanderlust that had plagued Hope her entire life.

"Charity will be fine. She and Thomas will soon be married. We will only be a train ride away. It will all work out, I promise. What do you say, Faith? Are you up for it?"

"It sounds to me like you've already made up your mind," Faith retorted. "You are going out west, no matter what I say. Isn't that so?"

Hope looked at her sister for a moment before she replied, "Yes, Faith, with or without you, I shall go west," she announced with a defiant tilt of her chin.

Faith cringed at the news. This would never have happened if Father were still alive. She ducked her head and tried to hide the tears threatening to fall. She could not imagine never again seeing her middle sister.

"Dear one, please come with me," Hope begged as she knelt and took her sister's delicate hands into her strong ones. "I'm afraid that if you stay behind, you'll end up being Charity's slave, living in her shadow and raising her children. It's not too late to have a life of your own, you know."

Suddenly, the door burst open, letting a gust of wind into the room. Charity made her entrance. There was no other way to describe it, as if she were a character in a play, taking the stage. Their youngest sister had bright blue eyes and hair that was a wild profusion of curls the color of a copper penny, which she always wore unbound. Charity paused for dramatic effect, waiting until she was certain she had her sisters' undivided attention. Slowly, she walked towards the kitchen table and sank into one of the chairs. Suddenly, she burst into tears then put her head down on her folded arms. Faith rushed to close the door.

"Charity dear, what is it? Hope, get her a cup of tea." Faith, ten years older than her youngest sister, had always mothered her.

Charity lifted her head and wailed. "H-he's g-gone!"

"He, who?" Hope asked, putting the kettle on to boil.

"Thomas, my fiancé!" Charity replied, annoyed that her sisters had not instantly realized the scope of her predicament. Faith and Hope's eyes met above their baby sister's head. They did not much care for Thomas. Besides being a flamboyant actor, they felt he was a rake and a bit of a scoundrel, but Charity had been taken by him ever since they'd performed together at the Boston Commons Theatre.

"Gone?" Faith asked, unable to comprehend why anyone would leave Boston. "Where did he go?"

"More importantly, why did he go?" Hope asked in that blunt way she had. She set the tea service on the table. "Tell us what happened, Charity, and start at the beginning."

Charity sat back and dabbed at her eyes. Faith knew that whatever happened, spinsterhood was not going to be Charity's fate. She was the loveliest of the three of them. Even now, her curls were perfectly arranged around her face as if she were posing for a portrait. Charity was a free spirit who did exactly as she pleased. She had not cared if appearing in theatrical productions had shocked the prudish matrons of Boston and made her an object of gossip. Faith only prayed that Charity had not been true to her name by being too lavish with her favors. She and Thomas had spent far too much time together without benefit of a chaperone.

"We were supposed to meet for breakfast at the café, but he never showed. I went by his boarding house, and the landlady said that he had taken his belongings and disappeared during the night. She said he owes her two months' back rent and her silver candlesticks are missing. She called the sheriff. I left before he arrived." Charity dissolved into hysterics. Her sisters had never seen her cry so hard.

"That scoundrel," Hope said, placing a cup of tea in front of Charity. "I knew he was no good. Men, you can't trust a one of 'em."

"Come now, dear," Faith urged as she put her arm around Charity's shaking shoulders. "You aren't helping," she scolded Hope, who just shrugged in response.

"Here, baby, drink your tea," Faith said. The three sisters gathered around the kitchen table. Faith and Hope patted Charity's hands and clucked sympathetically as she cried until she had no more tears left.

"I can't believe he left me without a word. Without a word and with our wedding just weeks away," Charity cried. "I loved him so. I am positively grief stricken."

"You would have had to postpone your wedding, anyway, because of Father's passing," Hope offered helpfully. This, however, did not seem to help at all. Faith and Charity just glared at her.

As fast as she'd started crying, Charity stopped. This was most unusual, her sisters knew. Charity liked to make the most of dramatic moments, drawing them out as long as possible. Suddenly, Charity stood, looking around the room with a critical eye as if she'd just remembered something.

"We are going to have a visitor any moment, sisters," she announced. Faith gasped and looked towards the parlor. The house was in no condition for callers. Charity caught her sister's look of dismay. "Don't worry, Faith. She won't be here long, and the house looks fine."

"Who is coming, dear?" Faith asked, trying to remain composed, but the panic in her voice gave her away. She didn't much care for visitors. If her sisters had callers, she would usually excuse herself and wait out their visit up in her room.

"Mrs. Reynolds, from the boarding house," Charity replied. Hope and Faith looked at one another; they knew no Mrs. Reynolds. "She saw how distraught I was over Thomas's disappearance. She said she wants to come to the house and talk to me. I presume it is about her mail order bride business." Faith and Hope stared blankly at her. "She arranges marriages between women in Boston with gentlemen out west. When I told her I had two single sisters, she was very eager to meet us all."

"I know what a mail order bride is, Charity, but I don't understand what any of this has to do with us," Hope protested as

Faith feverishly began to rush about the parlor, straightening and dusting.

"I know, I know, I'm not at all ready to talk about marrying someone else. I truly loved Thomas, and my heart is absolutely broken. But the matchmaker was persistent, and I didn't know what to do, so I invited her over. I just don't have the strength to deal with her, myself."

"Well, I guess it wouldn't hurt to hear what she has to say," replied Faith, trying to be supportive.

"I agree. On my way home, I thought about it. Perhaps a change of locations, at this point, would be ideal. I wouldn't want to stay in Boston after a broken engagement. It would be a scandal that could result in all three of us being ostracized socially," Charity said.

"I hardly think—" Hope began, but Charity quieted her with a glare. Hope was the last person to understand the rules of polite society.

"I know what those old biddies think of me, Hope. I'm too theatrical and not proper and, now, this broken engagement. I'm not going to lurk about in the shadows, ashamed to show my face. Maybe we should listen to what Mrs. Reynolds has to say with an open mind. Since we are losing the house, this could be the perfect solution for all three of us. I mean, really, what is left for us here in Boston?"

Hope nodded in agreement. "I have no problem with the idea of moving west. There's land out there, land for the grabbing. We could build something for ourselves. But explain to me, Charity, why do we need husbands?" Hope asked, confused.

"Let's let Mrs. Reynolds explain how it works," Charity replied. "Hope, go do something with your hair. I'll help Faith tidy up."

"What's wrong with my hair?" Hope asked.

"You look unkempt. Redo it."

Hope ambled off and returned a few minutes later and began to straighten the kitchen.

"I thought you were going to do something with your hair?" Faith said, looking at her.

"I did do something with my hair," Hope glowered. Her sisters were always trying to make her over. She couldn't help it if she had a thick mane of hair that was impossible to keep neatly pinned.

The girls had barely finished tidying when there was a knock at the front door. The three sisters stood in the foyer and straightened their skirts then checked their reflections in the small looking glass nearby. At a nod from Faith, Hope opened the door. Standing on the stoop was an attractive older woman. She smiled brightly at the three women and entered at Hope's invitation.

"Come in please, Mrs. Reynolds, I presume?" Hope asked. Mrs. Reynolds was colorful and well turned out, wearing a tartan plaid skirt and velvet jacket with a stylish hat atop her dark hair. Faith noted that her hair was a bit too dark, her lips a bit too red. Was the woman using cosmetics? Before she could ponder the question further, she was distracted by the large book under Mrs. Reynolds's arm.

"Hello, Mrs. Reynolds, thank you for coming," Charity said, stepping forward and steering Mrs. Reynolds towards their father's chair. "I was so distraught at the news about my fiancé that I don't think I would have regained my composure without your kind concern." Charity again began to cry. "I cannot believe that I was practically left at the altar."

"There, there, dear," Mrs. Reynolds said. "I am certain the young man found himself in difficult straits and did the only thing he could think to do. And, believe me, he will miss you much more than you will miss him. I do believe that you are one of the loveliest young ladies I have ever seen. I am certain that any of the men I represent would be thrilled to have you as a future bride."

Charity smiled at Mrs. Reynolds and dried her eyes, then she pulled Faith over in front of her. "Let me introduce my eldest sister, Faith. She's just twenty-eight, and I don't know why she insists on wearing her hair in that unflattering bun and dressing like a dowdy matron."

Faith tugged self-consciously at the lace collar on her charcoal grey dress. "Well, our father recently died, and we are in mourning," Faith said, looking pointedly at Charity's emerald green dress.

Charity continued on, seemingly without noticing. "I can assure you that Faith is quite pretty, once she lets her hair down," Charity went on.

Faith managed to smile, her lips a tight line.

"And this is Hope," Charity went on, walking over to stand by her other sister. "She is twenty-four, will turn twenty-five in May. She's the middle sister, even though most people take her to be the eldest. She's, well, she's strong and fit and a hard worker. And she's not bad to look at, either, in her own handsome way."

Hope glared at Charity, not liking being sized up like a prize pig.

"Oh my goodness," Mrs. Reynolds said, peering at all three girls through a set of opera glasses. "A house full of charming young women of marriageable age. Are you all interested in finding husbands out west?"

"No!" Faith blurted out. Hope shrugged, and Charity looked indifferent. Mrs. Reynolds knew that she had her work cut out for her. If she could convince one sister to move west, perhaps the other two would follow.

"You'll have to excuse my sister, Faith," Charity explained, concerned that she might have hurt Mrs. Reynolds feelings. "She's a bit timid, but I can assure you, she'll never stay behind in Boston by herself. Wherever we go, she will go. And she will make some gentleman a wonderful helpmate. Why, she single-handedly nursed our father through his final days."

Faith was shocked. Everything Charity had said with such assurance was true. She would follow her sisters anywhere. Was she that predictable?

"And you, Hope, are you ready to settle down and take a

husband?" Mrs. Reynolds asked, sizing up the large young woman. The girl did indeed have a handsome enough face, but she possessed a solid body and a set of shoulders like a prize fighter. This did not concern her, however, for most men preferred a woman with some meat on her bones. Settling the Great Plains was not for the frail of frame.

"To be honest, Mrs. Reynolds, I very much desire to relocate out west and get some land of my own. I'd like to prove that a woman can do her own homesteading."

"Yes, dear, and that's very commendable, by the way, but would it hurt to have a strong man as a partner? A rancher for you, I think. Yes, one with land available for homesteading nearby would be perfect." Hope reluctantly nodded. Mrs. Reynolds' suggestion did make sense.

"Come with me to the kitchen table, girls. Let's look through my book. I call it my 'Lonely Hearts book'. It is filled with pictures of gentlemen who are hoping to marry lovely, morally-upstanding young women, such as yourselves. There just aren't many women in the Great Plains area yet. It's known to be a spinsters' paradise. The place is filled with attractive men longing for wives."

"We are supposed to choose a man based on some grainy picture?" Hope asked, puzzled.

"Actually," Mrs. Reynolds replied, "I have personally interviewed and screened each one of these gentlemen and can answer any questions you may have."

"You have?" Hope asked, blinking in astonishment. "How many times have you traveled to Wyoming, Mrs. Reynolds?"

"For eight years now, I have made the journey with my young ladies every summer and then return to Boston in the fall with my book filled with new lonely hearts. Matchmaking is my calling. I feel it's much more humane to personally pair two lovely people together rather than to have a young lady answer some random ad in the newspaper. Choosing a husband is too important a matter to leave to happenstance."

"And what does this cost, if I may ask, Mrs. Reynolds?" asked Faith, afraid they would not be able to afford the woman's services.

"For my young ladies, nothing. The gentlemen retain my services, dear."

"But I'm afraid we wouldn't be able to afford the journey," Faith went on, trying to imagine how they would ever get themselves to Wyoming.

"The gentlemen purchase your train tickets. I already have them locked away, ready to give to sincere young women who will honor their commitments."

"Think of it, sisters! All we have to do is point to our choice and we are practically on our way," Charity said, beginning to sound enthusiastic. Faith looked with dismay from her to the matchmaker. Charity seemed to be actually considering the idea of becoming a mail order bride, but Faith was not at all certain about proceeding with this.

"If we should agree to this, we would want to be together in the same area," she said, anxiously wringing her hands.

"Of course, of course. All of the men in my book are from the Cheyenne part of the Wyoming Territory. Gather round now," she sang out gaily as she set the book in the middle of the table. All three girls took a seat, unable to resist seeing what sort of men would need a spouse so badly that they'd hire a matchmaker.

Mrs. Reynolds opened the book to the center. "Here are my ranchers. Do you see any that strike your fancy, Hope?"

Hope leaned over and looked doubtfully at the pictures. "I'm just not certain about this."

Mrs. Reynolds extended one long-nailed, manicured finger and pointed to a picture in the center of the page. "Here is a gentleman you might be interested in, Hope. This is Noble Enders, a rancher with a small daughter. Have you ever thought of being a mother, dear?" Hope sat back in silence, contemplating the question.

"Mr. Enders is thirty-two years of age," Mrs. Reynolds went on. "He's six-feet tall, of stocky build, solid and rugged. He told me that he is looking for a woman who is strong, sensible, and not afraid of hard work."

"Well, I am certainly all of those things," Hope replied, sitting bolt upright with a growing confidence.

Mrs. Reynolds read his advertisement out loud, finishing with, "And I should hope my future wife will know how to make biscuits and pies."

Hope laughed. "I suppose Faith could teach me the art of baking. But wouldn't having a husband make my future land his?"

"And his land would be yours, my dear. See how it all works out? He has one hundred forty-four acres and several hundred heads of cattle." Hope still looked doubtful, so Mrs. Reynolds turned her attention to Charity.

"A rugged, handsome cowboy for you, I think, Miss Charity. One who would tame your restless spirit?"

Charity's response shocked her sisters to the core.

"Pooh," she said, pushing the book away from her. "Tell me, Mrs. Reynolds. Who is the wealthiest man in that book of yours?"

"Charity!" Faith exclaimed. "Mrs. Reynolds is going to think we are gold diggers."

"I don't care what anyone thinks," said Charity with a toss of her head, which made her curls dance. "I have given up on romance. I gave my heart to Thomas, and where did it get me? Deserted and abandoned, that's where. If I'm going to uproot myself and move all the way to the Great Plains, I would want a better life awaiting me. Tell me, Mrs. Reynolds, are there any bankers in that book of yours?" she asked.

Faith shook her head and wished, not for the first time, that their parents were still alive. Their mother had died while all three girls were small, and their father had spent their formative years finding solace in the demon rum. Charity could have benefited from guidance and a strong hand, neither of which her older sisters had been equipped to provide.

Mrs. Reynolds didn't seem at all put off by Charity's

proclamation. "That's very sensible of you, dear." She took the book back and began looking carefully through it.

But Hope was not at all amused by her sister's proclamation. She began to scold Charity, who insisted there was nothing wrong in marrying for money. Mrs. Reynolds joined in, playing the peacemaker, and their voices escalated as the sisters argued with one another.

CHAPTER 2

*T*here was a knock on the front door heard only by Faith, who had stood and backed away from the table when her sisters began to argue. She opened the door, forgetting to be timid. On the stoop, she saw a large, grey-haired gentleman, tipping his hat.

"Pastor Hines!" Faith exclaimed. "How kind of you to come calling." She looked back over her shoulder fearfully at the colorful Mrs. Reynolds, deep in conversation with Hope and Charity. "To what do we owe the pleasure of this visit?" she asked, trying to step outside and pull the door shut behind her. But the minister held his ground. He tried to peer inside the house to see where all the raised voices were coming from, almost bumping heads with Faith in the process.

"Is everything all right? May I come in?" he asked, brushing past Faith and entering the house. The three ladies at the table grew silent, surprised to suddenly find a gentleman in their midst.

"I came to see how you young women are doing, now that your dear father has passed. And who is this lovely lady?" he asked as he entered the kitchen.

Mrs. Reynolds stood and held out her hand to the minister. "Enchanté," she said as he bowed to kiss it.

Faith blinked in astonishment. Were the pastor and matchmaker flirting?

"Hello, pastor, may I introduce Madame Reynolds?" Charity said. "She runs a mail order bride matchmaking service."

Faith thought she was going to faint on the spot. She had assumed her sisters would be as embarrassed as she about the reason for Mrs. Reynolds' visit, but apparently, that was not the case. Seeing what they were up to through the pastor's eyes suddenly made the entire affair seem unsavory.

"Pastor, please have a seat. Let me make you a cup of tea," she urged, seating him at the kitchen table.

"A matchmaker?" the pastor asked, raising a disapproving eyebrow as he settled heavily in his chair. "In the absence of these young ladies' father, I feel a responsibility to know what's going on here, Mrs. Reynolds. Please fill me in."

The matchmaker rose to the occasion, explaining in detail what sort of services she offered. "Pastor Hines, I represent a group of men who reside in the Wyoming Territory."

"Wyoming," the pastor said. "Ah, yes, where the Rockies meet the Great Plains. I hear it is beautiful country."

"It is and filled with lonely gentlemen ranchers. There's a cattle boom going on, you know. Each of the men in this book are successful and accomplished and well able to provide for a wife. There is a severe shortage of women in the northwest."

"And how thoroughly have you screened these gentlemen?" the pastor asked.

"I meet and converse extensively with each man before I take him on as a client. I won't have my genteel young Bostonian ladies answering random ads in the newspaper. I, myself, place the girls where I feel they will be the happiest."

"I understand that, but what does this have to do with the

Cummings girls? Which one of you is thinking of doing this?" the pastor asked, looking from one to the other.

Hope spoke up, "All three of us, if you must know, Pastor Hines. With father's passing and the loss of his pension, we can't afford to keep this house. I had thought about heading west, so we could homestead. Mrs. Reynolds, here, is providing a way for us to do that."

The pastor mopped his brow with his handkerchief and looked keenly at each girl. "Charity, what about you, engaged and soon to marry? What about your fiancé?"

Charity began to tell her sad tale, accompanied by the occasional tear running prettily down her cheek. By now, the story had escalated to her being abandoned 'while practically standing at the altar'.

Pastor Hines had known all three girls their entire lives and was not taken in by Charity's dramatics but did allow that he was sorry to hear her sad news. He drank up the contents of the little cup of tea Faith set before him, then he began to question Mrs. Reynolds again.

"What should happen if a young woman does not like her placement, once she meets her intended?"

"I travel with the girls and stay for the summer. If they are unhappy, at first, I keep them with me at the boarding house until they get to know their intended better or choose another," she replied.

"And if they should be content with their future spouses, when do the nuptials occur? Before any cohabitation, I would presume," the pastor said, looking skeptically at Mrs. Reynolds.

"Immediately upon arrival," Mrs. Reynolds replied, as if such a thing were perfectly normal. All three girls gasped and recoiled. Mrs. Reynolds turned to them. "It's quite jolly, girls. We all travel together, and upon arrival in Cheyenne, the gentlemen meet us at the train station. There is a procession to the chapel, which the townspeople gather to watch, throwing rose petals and calling out good wishes. Once at the church, the minister joins you, two-by-two, in holy matrimony in a big ceremony. Then you will ride with your spouse to your new home. Doesn't that sound lovely?"

The girls looked at one another. The pastor was asking sensible questions that hadn't even occurred to them.

He stood and began to speak as if he were delivering a sermon. "Before you proceed any further with this, I would be remiss if I didn't speak with you girls. Are there are no eligible young men here in Boston? While you girls may have no familial ties binding you to this area, you have a church family who is as concerned as I about your welfare. Going west is not your only option, I can assure you."

"We know that, pastor," Charity replied. "And we appreciate how supportive you have all been, calling on us and bringing meals after Father's passing. But we need to create futures for ourselves, and here, in Boston, the opportunity to do that has not presented itself. You have to admit that going west would solve a lot of our problems. All three of us would have increased opportunity to marry and have families of our own. And we won't be alone; we'll have each other."

"I had thought of getting the three of us out west to homestead," Hope added, trying to offer up another option that might meet with the pastor's approval. "Perhaps it would be better to work and save and purchase our own tickets?"

This got a reaction out of the pastor that none of them expected. "Absolutely not. If you girls plan to go west, I insist that each of you have a man waiting for you at the other end. The west is no place for a young lady on her own."

Mrs. Reynolds smiled delightedly; having the pastor's endorsement would help convince the girls that this is what they should do. "That is true, Pastor Hines. The west is no place for a young woman on her own. I have personally screened each of these men. They all are single, solvent, and have honorable intentions. I give you my word that no harm will come to these girls."

The pastor nodded and seemed to consider the matter. Finally, he spoke. "Choose now, young ladies. I am not leaving until you have made your choices and I have given my blessing." Pastor Hines crossed his arms and leaned back in his chair as if he truly intended to take up residence until the choices had been made.

The girls looked at each other, their eyes locking in silent communication as only sisters can. To have Pastor Hines and the church on their side would certainly make their move easier. Plus, he had known the girls their entire lives, and they each valued his wise counsel. Faith looked at the book, the book that possibly contained her and her sisters' futures.

"Pastor, would you say a prayer before we begin?" she asked.

The pastor raised his hands in prayer, asking for God's guidance as they made their choices. This made Faith feel infinitely better about the whole thing.

"Shall we start with the youngest, Miss Charity?" Madame Reynolds suggested.

Charity began to speak about what she wanted in a future husband. "He must be well able to provide a good life and to understand about my passion for the theater. By the way, is there a theater in Cheyenne?"

"To be honest, I am not certain, dear. But if there is not, I can't think of anyone better equipped than you to bring culture to the west. You could open a theater, or perhaps an opera house and form your own company of players."

Charity's eyes began to sparkle. Bringing culture to the natives sounded like the task she was born to.

Mrs. Reynolds turned to the front of the book. "I'm thinking a mature man who lives right in town. Nothing rural for you. Ah, here we are. Charity, this is Mr. Slade Miller. He has just turned forty, a widower with two grown children. He owns the mercantile in town. You could help him with his business and, of all the gentlemen in this book, he is the only one who mentioned an appreciation for the arts."

"He seems a bit old for Charity," Faith began as his picture was being passed around.

"That's just what Charity needs," hissed Hope. "A more mature man."

Faith could not argue with that.

"I think he sounds perfect," said Charity, handing the picture back to Mrs. Reynolds. All the women turned to Pastor Hines, who nodded his head, as if giving his blessing.

"And now, Hope, the rancher I've shown you would be ideal, I truly believe." Mrs. Reynolds said, turning the book back to the center page. "Currently, most of the land in Wyoming is owned by the government, but they are in the process of passing a Homesteading Act. And his ranch is quite rural, located several miles out of town. I'm certain there would be available land around it. But what you must know about Mr. Noble Enders is that he has an eight-year-old daughter. As the child's mother is deceased, you must prepare yourself to be a mother to her in every sense of the world."

Everyone turned to look at Hope, who looked even more uncertain than before.

"Here is a picture of the little girl," Mrs. Reynolds added, removing a photograph from an envelope inside the back cover. "I only show pictures of the children to women who have expressed an interest in their fathers."

Hope took the picture from her. It showed a child who could have been either a boy or girl. She wore her hair in a short bowl cut and was wearing a pair of overalls. She had her hand linked into a large dog's collar and was smiling jauntily into the camera. "The child's name is Grace, and she is a bit of a tomboy who could use the guidance of a mother figure," Mrs. Reynolds confessed, hoping that would not cause Hope to change her mind.

Instead, Hope smiled and said, "I believe I would quite enjoy having a daughter such as this."

Faith and Charity smiled at either other. They had never before seen such a gentle expression on Hope's face.

With Hope and Charity's futures settled, Mrs. Reynolds turned a practiced eye on Faith, the timid, oldest one. Faith was pretty enough with her pale skin and curly light brown hair pulled back into a bun, but she looked as if a strong wind would blow her away.

"I'm afraid there's nobody for me in that book of yours, Mrs. Reynolds," Faith said doubtfully, trying to tuck an escaped curl back into its bun.

"To be honest, Faith, most men want girls between the ages of eighteen and twenty-five, in the hopes of starting families. However, I am certain we can find a more mature man who would appreciate the companionship of a becoming young woman such as yourself. Tell me, what would your ideal man be like?"

"I don't particularly want children. They, well, they make me terribly nervous. Perhaps someone who has already raised their family and has a kind face?

Charity spoke up. "Choose a good man for our sister, Mrs. Reynolds. She took care of our ailing father for a very long time. She deserves some happiness in life."

Mrs. Reynolds smiled at Faith and then leafed through her book until she found a fatherly-looking man wearing furs.

"How about this gentleman, Faith? Mr. Jaan Anderson. He lives right on the outskirts of town in a log cabin he built with his own hands. His house sits on the edge of a tree farm. You'd love it there, Faith. It's an idyllic setting with a little stream running right near the house."

Faith studied the photograph. It showed a gentleman with white hair and a beard. He looked a bit wild, definitely rustic, with a wide smile on his face. She liked the picture. He wasn't posing as stiffly as the other gentlemen.

Hope looked over her shoulder and declared, "He's not for Faith." She snatched the picture out of Faith's hands and gave it back to Mrs. Reynolds.

"Why, Hope?" Faith asked, surprised by her sister's actions.

"He's too old. I won't have her nursing an old man through his declining years. She spent the last eight years doing that for our father. I want her to be with someone younger and livelier."

"Well, I like him," Faith said, snatching his picture back from Mrs. Reynolds. "You tell Mr. Anderson that I am on my way to his side, if he'll have me."

"You girls need to tell the gentlemen, yourselves. You must write letters to those you've selected and include a photograph and not a childhood photo, either. It's very important to men to have a picture of their intended to look upon. If you don't have any, go to the post office and get some made." Mrs. Reynolds knew when to cut and run. She stood and began to pack up her belongings. "I'll be back for your letters in a week. The train departs on May first. Be ready, girls. You may each bring a trunk and carry a satchel, but that is all. Remember, each of these men have fully stocked households, so you will only need your personal belongings."

As she rose, so did Pastor Hines. He turned to the girls and intoned, "A blessing upon each of you and your future unions. I shall be back by in a few days, girls, to see how you still feel about all of this." He turned to Mrs. Reynolds and extended an elbow, escorting her out of the door.

"Keep the photographs, girls," she called back over her shoulder.

"Well, I never," Hope said, watching Mrs. Reynolds speaking in a very animated way with the pastor.

"I do believe they were flirting," Faith said. "But that can't be true." The girls stood on the doorstep watching the pastor and the matchmaker walking down the street.

"Oh, yes, it can, sister," Charity said, amused. "Now come inside, girls. Let's start our letters to our gentlemen while it's fresh on our minds."

Instead, the girls sat in the parlor, wordlessly contemplating new futures.

Finally, Charity spoke again. "Think of it, sisters, adventure, romance, all set in the sweeping, majestic Great Plains. Ready-made homes and families, waiting for us to step in and take our places in their lives. We have less than ninety days to sell the house, clear it out and pack. In the meantime, we must get started on our letters."

"Yes but what if the gentlemen do not like us and refuse us?" Faith asked fearfully.

Hope looked at both of her sisters. "Why would they? We are healthy, attractive women with a sense of adventure. I should think they'd be glad to have us."

"What if someone else chooses them between now and then?" Faith asked.

"They won't," Charity said confidently.

"How can you be so certain?"

"We have their pictures! They are no longer in Mrs. Reynolds' book. They are ours now."

"Why, that's right," Faith said. Hope got up and moved to the desk to begin her letter. Charity put on her cloak.

"Where are you going?" Faith asked.

"To make an appointment to have our photographs done, of course. There is no time to waste." And with that, she was off.

Faith watched Hope working away on her letter. She knew she would need more time than her sisters to get used to the idea of the step they were about to take. She sat back in her chair, staring at the photograph of her future husband. Mr. Anderson was down on one knee in front of a fireplace with a rifle over his lap and a pile of furs beside him. Among other things, he appeared to be a trapper. She closed her eyes, trying to imagine living on the edge of a tree farm and being the wife of a man of action who went hunting and probably fished. That night, when she knelt beside her bed to say her prayers, there were three new names on her list. She prayed that God would keep Mr. Noble Enders, Mr. Slade Miller and Mr. Jaan Anderson safe and sound and that He would open the hearts of these men to accept their future brides.

CHAPTER 3

*T*he next three months flew by in a blur as Faith feared they would. They sold the house for more than the asking price. The new owners had wanted the furnishings, so all the girls had to remove from the house would be their personal items. Faith walked through the rooms, saying goodbye to each familiar piece of furniture and reminiscing aloud about its history.

"Stop, Faith," Charity finally said in exasperation. "We did not personally accumulate any of this furniture. It's old and worn and not worth mourning the loss of."

Faith smiled sadly. That was not entirely true. She remembered her father building Charity's cradle and how excited her parents had been at the gift of a new, late-in-life child. Their happiness had ended with the death of their mother when Charity was just four years of age. She realized that she was saying goodbye to her childhood and their way of life. Boston had been a magical place to grow up in. Surely, Wyoming couldn't be half so wonderful? So many times, Faith had wanted to call off the upcoming move, but then the thought would come to her, what would they be doing now if they weren't heading west? The three of them would certainly be facing separation and possible homelessness. The thought was too much to bear, so she put it out of her mind and kept her doubts to herself.

One day, Hope burst into the house with important news. "Sisters, we are going to have some money left over after the mortgage is paid off. It's not a great deal but, split three ways, we will have enough to comport ourselves with dignity throughout our journey west and pay the homesteading deposit. And here's the best part—we can afford our own train tickets. That way, we won't be at the mercy of the gentlemen waiting at the other end."

"Whatever do you mean?" Faith asked. She wasn't sure she liked this new development.

"I mean, sister dear, that we use the gentlemen's tickets to get ourselves there, and once we see them face to face, if we don't like 'em, we simply reimburse them for the price of our tickets and walk away."

"But, Hope, you can't be serious. We have already written to these men and made promises. They have undoubtedly shown our pictures to their friends and loved ones. It would be so rude to spurn them after this," Faith said, pleading with her sister to reconsider.

Hope hadn't appeared to be listening. She was standing at the front window, hands on her hips, looking out towards a future of independence.

But when Faith added, "Why, little Grace is probably looking forward to having a mother once more," Hope turned to her.

Faith could see a moment of hesitation flicker over her sister's face. Hope, who had always been determined to do things her own way and conquer the future on her own terms, seemed to have been touched by the photo of the little girl who needed a mother. Faith was pleased to see that, for once, Hope was thinking of someone besides herself, but then Charity chimed in.

"If there are all these men out west desperate for wives, why shouldn't we pick and choose? Why should we be tied to someone we've exchanged letters with once or twice? Why not meet them all and then decide whom we are most attracted to?"

Faith sighed in exasperation. Neither loyalty nor keeping one's word seemed to matter to her independent sisters.

"You two can do as you please, but I shall keep my word to Mr. Anderson. I intend to take my place at his side as his wife and helpmate. I have no intention of being free with my favors while trying to decide whom I might be attracted to, whatever that means. Life is about so much more than attraction, Charity. How long do you think that would last?"

Both of her sisters ignored her and began to discuss how to get their financial windfall safely west. There had been news in the paper recently about a rash of train robberies. Faith had sewn a pouch to wear hidden in her waistband close to her body, Charity talked about sewing large coins into her bodice, but Hope had decreed that she had a much better plan but would not share the details.

Faith took Hope into the kitchen to prepare their dinner. Under her tutelage, Hope had managed to produce some lovely cakes, a couple of savory pies, and a halfway decent pan of biscuits.

"The key to successful baking is putting love into it. As you mix and measure, think about those you are baking for. Tonight, you are again making biscuits, and tomorrow, we will start on bread baking."

"Noble didn't write anything about baking bread," Hope retorted. "He just mentioned pies and biscuits."

"Well, how do you think you are going to get bread? It goes without saying that you need to know how to make it," Faith replied, losing her patience. "And have you thought about the fact that your future husband owns a ranch? You will no doubt, on occasion, be called upon to feed the ranch hands. Even if they normally heat up their own meals, during certain busy times, you may need to feed them all. I understand a lot of beans are eaten out west. I've had this bowl soaking all day. You will make it into our dinner."

Hope, cowed by the impatience in her sister's voice, buckled down, and that night, they dined on a delicious bowl of beans and biscuits.

"If this is how they eat our west, I'm going to like it there," Charity stated afterwards, and Hope beamed with pride.

All too soon, it was time to go to church for their going away party. As the girls walked down the sidewalk, they reveled in the warm night air. Spring had definitely settled in, signaling that it was time to be putting their trunks on the train to head west. In fact, they had sent their trunks on ahead that very day to be put on tomorrow's train. Faith worried aloud about keeping her composure as they said goodbye to their church family.

"They are good people; that's for certain," said Hope.

"And we will meet many more good people in Wyoming," added Charity.

"I'm sure you're right," agreed Faith, although her tone of voice betrayed her doubt. Once they reached the church, the doors flew open, and she and her sisters were hugged and petted by a crowd of people. Some thought their upcoming adventure too wonderful for words, others could only shake their heads and express concern. But all in all, it was a soul-warming gathering around a table groaning with delicious food.

After everyone had eaten, Pastor Hines stood to speak and announced that he had already written to the pastor in Cheyenne and sent a letter of recommendation for the three girls. He had received a response and read it to the congregation.

"The township of Cheyenne can only be improved by the addition of the Cummings sisters. We very much look forward to welcoming them to our parish upon their arrival," the pastor in Wyoming had written. Pastor Hines went on to say that Pastor Gregory, the minister in Wyoming, had included a photograph of the congregation in front of the church, taken during last year's fourth of July picnic. The picture was passed around and exclaimed over.

Faith instantly felt reassured that there were indeed good people waiting for them in Wyoming. She wiped away a tear of relief and could finally envision herself and her sisters walking down the sidewalks of Cheyenne, Wyoming.

The next morning, Faith was up while it was still dark. She made a pot of coffee, the smell waking her sisters.

"Come along, girls, or the train will leave without us," she called. The day had arrived to begin their journey to Wyoming.

Hope came downstairs, wearing traveling clothes and a heavy pair of boots.

"Are you going to tell us where you have hidden the bulk of our money?" Charity asked.

Hope lifted up her left foot. "Remember the sole on this boot that was flapping loose? I took it to the shoe repair and had the money sealed inside of it."

"Very clever," Charity said sarcastically. "How are we supposed to get to it in an emergency?"

"We aren't. The money will be safely hidden until we get to our destination and can have the sole cut open. I'm not worried about emergency money; we are each carrying enough to get us through the trip. Spend freely at the beginning, sisters. Eat well in the dining car. I did a study at the library; train travel is perfectly safe until we near Wyoming. That way, if we are robbed during the final leg of our journey, we won't lose much."

Faith rinsed out the coffee pot and set it on the stove top.

"We are leaving it behind?" Charity asked, surprised.

"I'm sure the new owners will be pleased to find it here," Faith replied.

"And if we need one in Wyoming, we can purchase it there," Hope added.

Faith did not point out that they would no longer be living together once they reached Wyoming. She did not trust herself to say those painful words aloud. The three girls had always been 'we', united together to survive growing up in an unhappy household. Soon, they would branch out and form three separate households. Faith began to bustle about so that her sisters could not see her distress.

They were soon on their way to the train station and arrived there in plenty of time. They instantly spotted Mrs. Reynolds fluttering about like a mother hen as she gathered a group of young women around her. Faith counted their numbers. There were a dozen women besides herself and her sisters. There was another set of two sisters, small and dark, who did not appear to speak English. Faith's eye was caught by a tall, slender, pale blonde who stood apart from their group speaking to a young man. In front of everyone, he fell to one knee and held out an engagement ring. Faith watched, fascinated, as the girl looked sadly at the young man and shook her head no.

Faith turned to say something to her sisters, but Hope was no longer at her side. She was down the tracks, supervising as their trunks were being loaded on the train, making sure their belongings made it on board. Charity was animatedly speaking with Mrs. Reynolds, oblivious to the romantic moment happening just steps away. When Faith turned back, the young man was standing and holding the girl's hand, but she pulled away and went to stand by Mrs. Reynolds. Why would she be traveling west if she had a suitor right here in Boston, Faith wondered?

Faith looked away, studying the young women who would be their traveling companions. They came in all shapes and sizes but most appeared to be in Mrs. Reynolds's target range of eighteen to twenty-five. Faith was, by far, the oldest of the group.

There was quite a crowd gathered at the platform to say goodbye to the young women. Faith saw a particularly young-looking girl, crying her eyes out. The child couldn't have been a day over eighteen. Her mother was crying, and her father, with sad eyes, pretended to be gruff. Faith overcame her shyness enough to approach the young woman.

"Are you traveling with us to Wyoming?" she asked kindly, and the girl nodded. Faith put her arm around her and promised her parents that she would personally see to it the girl reached Cheyenne safely. That seemed to help; both parents managed an appreciative smile as the girl turned to Faith and began to cry on her shoulder.

"All aboard!" the porter called, and everyone began to pile on the train.

Faith took a seat with the young girl as Hope and Charity sat across from them. She watched as Mrs. Reynolds followed the rest of the girls onboard. They rushed to the windows and began calling to their loved ones on the platform, waving white handkerchiefs out of the open windows. Faith noticed that the tall, pale blonde girl went to the doorway before the doors closed and took one last look around. It appeared that it was easier for her to leave behind her besotted admirer than it was for her to leave Boston. Faith knew just how she felt.

"Thank goodness, no one from the church came to say goodbye," said Charity. "I'd prefer to remember everyone as they were last night at our goodbye party."

"Who is your young friend, Faith?" Hope asked, staring curiously at the young girl who was crying too hard to even wave goodbye.

"I don't know; we haven't had a chance to introduce ourselves," Faith replied. Just then, the train whistle blew as it lurched into motion, and then came the sound of the wheels turning, beginning to pick up speed. Faith held on to the seat tightly. The two small, dark sisters both shrieked and moaned, clearly frightened by the movement of the train. But Faith was distracted by her young friend, who had instantly stopped crying. Her face lit up with a big smile as they pulled out of the station.

"Hello," she said to Faith, Hope and Charity. "My name is Doreen, and it's my birthday."

"And how old are you?" Hope asked.

"I'm nineteen-years-old and so happy to be getting away from home, I can't tell you."

"Well, happy birthday, Doreen," said Faith. "I was worried about you. You and your mother were so upset."

"It's hard to say goodbye, but it had to be done. I'm my parents' oldest child and a second mother to my siblings. You see, there are lots of little ones at home, and to tell you the truth, I'm tired of taking care of them. I'm marrying a man who doesn't have any children. I intend that the next babe I have to heft upon my hip will be my very own."

Faith laughed and turned to look around. She was about to point out the tall, pale blonde to her sisters, when Mrs. Reynolds came to the front of the train car and began to speak.

"Welcome, young ladies, look around. These girls are your future friends and neighbors, and we are a big enough group to have been given our own train car. See, you already know people in Cheyenne. I have a big announcement, girls, Wyoming has just been ratified and will soon be made a state. There is a cattle boom going on, as well as a baby boom, and the town is growing by leaps and bounds. Cheyenne now has two post offices, three churches, and its own doctor."

The girls cheered, agreeing that this seemed to be a good omen, indeed.

"Why don't we introduce ourselves? I'll start out. My name is Jeanette Reynolds and, like most of you, I was born and raised in Boston. Ten years ago, I went to visit my sister out west after my poor husband died; may he rest in peace." At this, several of the young women bowed their heads, some making the sign of the cross.

"There, I met many lonely gentlemen. I knew several single ladies back in Boston, so I made it my mission to bring the two groups together. This is my ninth trip to Wyoming, and I am personally responsible for over a hundred weddings. Hundreds of babies have been born of these unions, and the vast majority of these marriages have been wildly successful. Faith dear, will you go next, since you are my senior bride?"

Faith smiled. Mrs. Reynolds had managed to avoid using the world 'oldest'. Before she could get nervous and tongue-tied, Faith stood and introduced herself, thinking that perhaps some of the younger brides might need her for moral support.

"I am Faith Cummings. I'm traveling with my two younger sisters, Hope and Charity. Our parents are deceased, and we felt that this offered us a chance for new lives. I've lived in Boston my entire life and never thought of making such a journey, but here I am. My special skill is baking, especially pies, and I'd be glad to share my recipes with any of you. I also knit and garden and enjoy canning. I am heading west to marry Mr. Jaan Anderson, and we'll live in his log cabin, which is on the edge of a tree farm." Suddenly, Faith realized what she was doing—public speaking. Her face drained of color, and she sat down abruptly.

Charity patted her hand and leaned over to whisper, "It's amazing what you can do when you get your mind off of yourself."

When it was Hope's turn to speak, she became an advocate for women's rights, encouraging the young woman to take advantage of the Homesteading Act that was up for a vote in the capital. The girls looked puzzled. This was not at all the reason they were moving west.

Next, it was Charity's turn. By the time she finished sharing how she had been stood up at the altar and how Mrs. Reynolds had been her savior, showing her the way to a new future, the girls in the group were swarming around and comforting her, wondering aloud how such a pretty girl could possibly have been betrayed by a no-good scoundrel like that Thomas.

After Charity, the tall, pale blonde stood up and spoke. She introduced herself as Helga Helstrom, of Norwegian descent. She shared that she, too, had been engaged but discovered that her young man had cheated on her—with her sister, no less. She had heard about Mrs. Reynolds and had run all the way to the boarding house to sign up to go west.

"I'm sorry," Faith said, raising her hand. "Was that the young man who proposed to you at the station?"

"Yes," Helga said, nodding her head sadly. "He swears never to do such a thing again, but how could I possibly trust him? And I can't stand to even look upon my sister."

The girls all nodded their heads, agreeing with her. Faith suspected that Helga was the next oldest bride. She seemed plain, at first sight, but she had a dignity that made her appear attractive.

Next to pop up to speak was little Doreen. She was tiny but curvaceous and had a headful of brown, frizzy curls with a sprinkling of freckles across her nose. "Today is my birthday, and I just turned nineteen, although I know I look younger. My parents immigrated to America from Scotland. I am the oldest of twelve children, and my mother cried like a babe when I left. I was the second mother around the house, but I needed to get away, far, far away. I want my own life, and I want my own wee ones. My future husband is a ranch hand named Dobie, and he wrote that he's been wanting a wife something fierce. He's tall and handsome, and I just can't wait to get to Wyoming."

The women all wished her a happy birthday and smiled at the idealistic young girl's excitement. Faith said a silent prayer that Dobie would be everything Doreen could possibly want.

Next, were the two sisters who spoke little English. Mrs. Reynolds introduced them to the group, and all the women smiled encouragingly. She said that the girls were not only sisters, they were twins. Faith was puzzled. They didn't look at all alike; one was taller, and the shorter one was prettier, but they did look like sisters. Mrs. Reynolds went on to say that the girls were from Spain and they had become orphaned on the ship to America and were staying at her boarding house. She had found a translator and spoken to the girls, who were quite impoverished. She was taking them to Wyoming to marry twin brothers, who were from Mexico and, together, owned a ranch. The girls would not be separated.

A tear came to Faith's eye; it was the perfect solution. The girls would have security and provide their young men with able help. Faith looked at Mrs. Reynolds with new eyes. She was a good woman, truly providing a most important service. Those girls would probably have become overworked, underpaid servants living in poverty in Boston. Instead, they were to become rancher's wives, working their own land with husbands they'd be able to communicate with.

The rest of the girls spoke, one by one. Red-headed Molly felt she was a burden to her single mother. She was marrying a farmer and hoped to send for her mother after she got settled. Bespectacled Edith was a teacher and a writer and quite overcome at the thought that there was a handsome cowboy waiting for her in Wyoming. She blushed and fanned herself whenever she spoke of him. Blonde Alma had nursing training and was going to marry and work with the town doctor. The rest had similar stories—they were orphaned or a burden to their families and seeking new lives. Faith marveled at the Lord God's hand in all of this. She silently spoke to Him, expressing gratitude for being a part of this adventurous group.

So that was the fifteen of them, ranging in age from nineteen to twenty-eight. Some were slender, some were stout, some plain and some beautiful, but each was special in her own way. Mrs. Reynolds praised her brides for their adventurous spirits, calling them 'angels with wings'.

This time, Charity was the one who snickered as Faith glared at her. Mrs. Reynolds then made the unfortunate mistake of asking if anyone had any questions.

Hope's hand shot up.

"Yes, dear?" the matchmaker asked.

"How many times, on your journeys to Wyoming, has your train been robbed, Mrs. Reynolds?"

The matchmaker blanched, and several of the young women gasped and began to murmur. Faith watched Charity roll her eyes at this. Hope often shocked and alienated people with her blunt manner.

Mrs. Reynolds waved her arms, shushing everyone. "That doesn't happen much anymore, dear," she assured one and all, but Hope would not be dismissed.

"On the contrary, Mrs. Reynolds, there has been a rash of recent robberies. By my estimation, the most dangerous leg of our journey will lie about a day out from Wyoming."

Mrs. Reynolds sighed and decided that there was nothing to do except discuss the unpleasant matter. "Actually, I *have* encountered train robbers."

Several of the young ladies gasped at this.

"I found them to be young men doing it as much for a sense of adventure as for the treasures they gather. Girls, if we are indeed stopped by train robbers, sit still, stay calm and give them whatever they want. Do you understand? If you have any valuable, sentimental pieces of jewelry, hide them well away. Most robbers just want cash and are quickly on their way. Keep the bulk of your money hidden away, keep your expendable cash in your purse and give them that. Don't make eye contact. Remain calm and polite. I'll go over all this again after we leave Cleveland. And now, let's put that unpleasantness aside and sing."

She led the girls in a patriotic song, desperately trying to keep them from panicking.

"Hope, for heaven's sake! Why on earth would you talk about such a thing?" Faith scolded.

Hope shrugged. "Odds are, it's going to happen. We might as well prepare ourselves."

"Well, for Heaven's sake, don't tell anyone where our money is hidden," Charity hissed.

"Of course, I wouldn't." Hope shrugged. "The only reason I told you two was in case something happened to me. You needed to know."

Faith was quite surprised at how elegant train travel was. The dining car had tablecloths and waiters dressed in black with white napkins draped over their arms. The girls ordered nice dinners, but Faith was watching the two Spanish sisters. They huddled together and hadn't ordered. They looked around with wide eyes as dinners were brought to the tables. Faith relaxed when she saw two plates of food being set in front of them. Clearly, Mrs. Reynolds was taking good care of them. She watched as they shoveled the food into their mouths as if they were starving. Well, hopefully, those days were over for the two new immigrants.

Charity saw Faith watching the two sisters. "It's been good for you to get out, Faith. You do well when you are thinking of others, rather than dwelling on your own fears and foibles."

"I hope Mr. Anderson will treat you well and help you feel safe," Hope added, nodding in agreement with what Charity had said.

"I have been praying for all three gentlemen. I hope we will all have good husbands," Faith said.

"It can't be any worse than what we are leaving behind," Helga interrupted. She had joined the three sisters at their table. Doreen was off chatting with some of the younger brides.

Charity was studying Helga, probably trying to master her accent, Faith suspected, and that sad but dignified way she had of carrying herself.

"Have you ever acted?" Charity asked casually.

"Acted?" Helga asked, startled. "What is that—acted?"

"You know, appeared in a play. I, myself, am an actress," Charity said.

Helga looked taken aback. Well, Faith thought, of course, she was shocked. One didn't meet a woman who admitted to being an actress every day. She remembered the first time Charity had called herself an actress. Up until then, Faith had hoped the appearances her little sister had made in various plays over the years had been just a hobby. It alarmed her to think that Charity actually thought of herself as a professional thespian. *What next?* she had often wondered. Would Charity start traveling around the country, doing plays? She had begun to take on a theatrical look as she'd entered her teens, with her red hair and colorful dresses. She drew jealousy from her classmates, and the mothers had gossiped about her. Faith couldn't stand that happening to her little sister, but Charity didn't seem to mind. She just followed her own path, not caring about the repercussions.

The three sisters settled down then and began to eat their dinners as they looked out the window at the occasional light flashing by.

CHAPTER 4

The day came when they left the safety of the mid-west and began the final leg of their journey. The train travel became more rustic. There were fewer train cars, for one thing, and the brides no longer had their own compartment. The windows were opened as the weather grew warmer, and soon, there was a fine layer of dust covering everything. There was no longer a dining car. The girls bought food when the train stopped and shared it with each other. Fruits, vegetables and bread and meat were standard fare. Some of the young ladies seemed to be running out of funds. Mrs. Reynolds and Faith did their best to make sure that everyone had enough to eat.

On their last day of travel before reaching Wyoming, the sisters agreed that their journey had been a safe and uneventful one.

Just as Hope declared they seemed to have avoided train robbers, Charity pointed out the window off in the distance. "Look. What's that?"

All of the brides rushed to the windows in time to see a cloud of dust rising up in the distance. To their horror, they realized it was coming closer.

"Train robbers!" Hope shouted.

They were able to make out figures on horseback, four or five of them. The Spanish girls began to wail, just as the train brakes began to screech. Faith looked around at the commotion breaking out as the brides began to rush around, hiding their things.

"Is this a scheduled stop?" Charity, cool as a cucumber, asked the porter.

"No, something must be lying across the tracks up ahead."

"I was afraid of this," Mrs. Reynolds said, looking worriedly out the window.

"Why?" asked Hope.

"Because this is a transport train; it's carrying a load of cash. The good thing is that the robbers are usually satisfied with that."

"Then let's pray they leave the passengers alone," Faith whispered.

But it didn't play out quite like that. No sooner had the train come to a complete stop than their car was taken over by a handful of dusty, young men in cowboy gear with bandanas covering their faces. The men smelled like horse and seemed wild-eyed and dangerous. The brides all froze in place except for the two Spanish sisters, who clutched each other and cried. One of the cowboys approached the two but walked on by, probably put off by their ragged apparel.

"Is this a mail order bride transport?" another fellow asked, upon seeing all the anxious young ladies standing in a line with their hands up. The fellow, who appeared to be the leader, walked up and down the aisle, looking at each young woman. Helga looked as if she was about to swoon, but Charity stood up to him.

"None of your business. Take what you want and go, you animals."

"Animals, are we?" He walked up to her and took her chin in his hand, tilting her face until she was glaring defiantly into his eyes.

"Leave her alone!" Hope cried. She lunged at the fellow, but Mrs. Reynolds and Faith held her back.

"Now, now, everyone, just stay calm and cooperate, and you

have my word that no one will get hurt. Now give us your money," said the ringleader, still staring into Charity's eyes. The brides, weeping, each took money out of their wrist bags and handed it to the men. The robbers moved up and down the aisle, asking for any jewelry they saw. None of the brides wore jewelry, thanks to Mrs. Reynolds' warning to hide it.

FINALLY, the men started to leave, but then Charity's robber lowered his bandana and leaned into her, stealing a kiss. Hope began to shout at the man, but Charity, oddly, didn't fight him. It even seemed as if she leaned into him, kissing him back. He chucked her under the chin and then walked past Hope, who snarled at him. Then he was gone; they were all gone. Everyone stayed frozen in place, not daring to breathe as the robbers continued up and down the train cars.

Eventually, Mrs. Reynolds said, "Thank God," as the men could be seen mounting their horses. The girls ran to the windows and watched them ride away. Everyone sat down, and several of the women dissolved into tears. Mrs. Reynolds bustled up and down the aisle, wiping tears dry and reminding the girls that they had been lucky. No one had gotten hurt.

"Unfortunately, that was your first encounter with cowboys, but rest assured, most are not like those fellows. I can assure you that most men in the west are upstanding, with high morals."

The porter came through, making sure no one had been injured. He reported that the track was being cleared and the train would soon begin again.

"Stop crying, dear," Mrs. Reynolds said to one of the Spanish brides.

"Para de llorar," Miss Edith, the former schoolmarm, said to the smaller sister. Everyone looked at her in surprise.

"You speak Spanish?" Mrs. Reynolds asked.

"I studied it in school but don't remember much," explained Edith.

"We got off relatively easily," Mrs. Reynolds spoke up so all the brides could hear. "The porter will come back through to take your statements, so try to remember anything that would help the authorities identify those men. Did you see their hair or eyes or any distinguishing marks? Perhaps you heard one call another by name? Any information at all would be helpful."

"Do you really believe we got off easily?" Hope asked Mrs. Reynolds.

"Yes, indeed. I have seen women made to remove various items of clothing as the scoundrels looked for hidden valuables."

"Did anyone lose all of their money?" Hope asked, standing to face the girls. No one owned up to that happening, but when she sat back down, she found Faith in tears.

"What is it, sister?" she asked, concerned.

"I had a rather large coin on me that the thieves took. I hadn't had time to hide it away after our last stop. I've lost over half my money."

"Not to worry," Hope said, patting Faith's hand. "We still have the bulk of our money safely hidden away, and Charity and I will split what we have left with you. Are you all right, Charity?"

"Of course, of course, it was only a kiss," Charity said. She truly seemed to have gotten through her ordeal without trauma. "The best part is, he didn't take any of my money."

"He didn't?" Hope asked. Then she began to laugh. "I do believe you hypnotized him with your feminine wiles."

"Well, he was very handsome," Charity said, smiling.

"Charity!" Faith was shocked at her sister's reaction. "You found the train robber attractive? For Heaven's sake, what is going to become of you, little sister?"

Everybody was on edge that night, and after giving their statements, the sisters tried to sleep. Faith was not at all able to settle down, still worrying about the lost money. As the sun rose in the morning, the porter came through, announcing that they would reach the Cheyenne station in a couple of hours. The brides began to freshen up. Mrs. Reynolds walked up and down the aisle giving the girls a pep talk.

"Look as pretty as you can, girls. Your husbands are about to see you for the first time. Today is your wedding day," she sang as the girls began to bustle with excitement. "I know you are worn out from your journey, but you are young women and will soon recover."

Faith leaned over and whispered to Hope and Charity, "You girls aren't still thinking of jilting your intended at the train station, are you?"

Hope didn't answer, but Charity replied in the affirmative. "I have no intention of handing myself over to some man I've only written to once or twice. If I don't like the looks of him, I'll just hand him the cash for my train ticket, which I have right here," she said, patting her pocket. "And I'll be on my way."

Faith's heart sank. She hoped that Mr. Slade Miller would not end up with his heart broken. Charity became still, and then Faith realized that she hadn't said much of anything since the robbery. It was all most unusual, since Charity liked to milk dramatic situations. Instead, she had been as quiet as a mouse, just staring out the window and curling her hair around her finger.

Soon enough, they were pulling into the train station. Faith peeked out the window. The station was full of people milling about, which she thought was odd since there weren't that many people left on the train.

"All those people aren't here just for us, are they?" she asked Mrs. Reynolds. The matchmaker glanced out the window and affirmed that they were indeed.

"I told you all, it's quite festive when the bride train pulls in to town. The townspeople look forward to it all year." As if on cue, music began to play.

"It's a band," exclaimed one girl.

"And there are people holding up signs," said another.

The door opened in the train car. The girls had been trying to brush each other's jackets off, but a thin layer of dust continued to cover everything. Mrs. Reynolds stepped out on the top of the steps that led down from the train car. A cheer arose; apparently, everyone knew who she was. The girls could see her trying to quiet the crowd by waving her hands until she could speak.

"The bride train has indeed arrived, and I have no less than fifteen lovely young ladies on board. If the gentlemen who received letters will line up at the foot of the stairs, I will bring the brides out, one by one."

Mrs. Reynolds called for Helga. The crowd grew silent as she stepped bravely out of the train car and was helped down the steps by a tall, bespectacled young man who looked upon her as if she were a goddess. Helga smiled prettily at him, and he took her in his arms for a kiss. A cheer arose from the crowd.

Faith, inside the train, turned scarlet watching this unfold. The entire scene was a little too public for her taste. But the girls were rushing the door and starting down the steps, and bedlam broke out. Faith sat in the window and watched as little Doreen was the next down the steps. A very tall young man with ears that stuck out stepped forward. Doreen looked up at him and giggled and threw her arms around him. Faith was pleased to see that they seemed delighted with one another.

Mrs. Reynolds led the two Spanish girls to their Mexican husbands. At first, the girls stood shyly, looking down at the ground, but then the men began to speak to them in Spanish and the girls came to life. Soon, the four of them were chattering away in Spanish, the girls suddenly smiling and vivacious.

Charity stepped out of the train and stood at the top step, and the crowd stilled once more as all faces turned towards her. The crowd parted, and Mr. Slade Miller stepped forward, looking both older and handsomer than he had appeared in his picture. Faith recognized him as he removed his hat. He looked up at Charity as if she were a vision sent from Heaven above. Then Faith saw Charity rush down the steps and take the man by the hand, pulling him into the crowd. From her vantage point, she could see the man's face as Charity spoke to him, apparently refusing him. She saw her try to hand the man money for her ticket, but he turned and walked away, clearly very angry. Faith wanted to cry. Her little sister had clearly rebuffed the handsome man, the only person in Mrs. Reynolds's Lonely Hearts book who had expressed an 'interest in the arts'. Faith shook her head sadly. What would become of her little sister now?

Hope helped Faith to her feet and pushed her on ahead out of the train car. Faith looked around, but there was no white-haired gentleman waiting to greet her. She went down the steps and stood back; perhaps he hadn't arrived at the station yet? She turned and saw Hope standing at the top of the stairs and watched as a large stocky man stepped up to her. He put his hands around Hope's waist and lifted her off the steps as if she weighed nothing. Mr. Noble Enders was quite handsome, with a wide brow and brown eyes and straight black hair. As Faith anxiously watched, she saw Hope smile up at him then bend over and greet a little brunette girl who was holding a handful of wilted daisies. She took the flowers from the little girl and kissed her on the cheek then linked arms with her Mr. Noble Enders. Tears of happiness came to Faith's eyes. Hope seemed to be honoring her commitment to her fiancé and future stepdaughter.

Faith was dabbing at her eyes, but then she noticed Mrs. Reynolds speaking to a group of official-looking men. There was a man who was clearly the sheriff in town, judging by the badge on his vest. There was also a black-collared minister, Pastor Gregory, whom she recognized from the picture postcard he had sent with his congregation in front of the church, as well as two other men. The group turned and began to walk towards Faith. Suddenly, she knew in her heart of hearts that something was terribly wrong. Something had happened to Mr. Anderson; that's why he wasn't at the station. In a heartbeat, as if she, too, had sensed something amiss, Charity was beside her and the group was taken away from the noisy crowd inside the cool quiet of the train station.

Mrs. Reynolds began to speak. "Faith, there is sad news about your intended."

"Mr. Anderson?" Faith asked. She was by now in such a state that she was having trouble hearing through the roaring in her ears.

"Yes, dear, Sheriff McKenna will tell you what happened."

The sheriff stepped up, his hat in his hands, and introduced the three men beside him. "Miss Cummings, this is the banker, Mr. Walden, Pastor Gregory, and Doctor Neesan."

Faith looked at the men; they all looked very solemn. She swallowed hard and stood stock still as the sheriff continued speaking.

"It is our sad duty to inform you that Mr. Anderson passed away just last Friday."

Faith gasped and began to sway on her feet. Charity put her arm around her waist and leaned into her, holding her up.

The doctor spoke. "He passed peacefully in his sleep. There was no warning. Sometimes, these things just happen," he added, shrugging helplessly.

Pastor Gregory added, "I want you to know, dear lady, that he had your picture on the stand beside his bed. He had told everyone how happy he was to have such a 'pretty little gal' coming to share his life. When we discovered he had passed, it was too late to send word. You had already begun your journey."

Faith began to cry, dabbing at her eyes with her handkerchief as Charity patted her arm.

Finally, the banker spoke. "This is the sum total of his savings, Miss Cummings. We all agreed that you should have it." He held out a bag of coins. "There will be more when his house sells." Faith was too stunned to reach for it, but Charity took it and spoke for her.

"Thank you, all of you, for delivering this difficult news to my sister."

The sheriff spoke up once more. "While there is enough in that bag of coins to purchase passage on the next train out of here, it is our hope that you'll stay on in Cheyenne, Miss Cummings. There are plenty of good men who would love to make your acquaintance. Once you've had time to recover, of course."

Mrs. Reynolds said, "Faith is here with her two sisters. I can assure you that she will stay on at the boarding house with me. She won't return to Boston if her sisters are here."

Faith once more wondered if she was really that predictable? It was true. She would never go back to Boston if her sisters were in Wyoming. She watched the men take their leave, and for a moment, she thought she was going to faint, but Charity had a firm hold on her and Mrs. Reynolds took her other elbow.

"Faith, there will be time to grieve later. Right now, your sister, Hope, is on her way to the church to marry her Mr. Enders. You will never forgive yourself if you miss it."

Charity agreed, and between them, they led Faith out the door and along behind the crowd of people heading down the street. Just as Mrs. Reynolds had promised, people were throwing rose petals and shouting out their good wishes. The band was playing; the little white church had been decorated with bunting and flowers. They managed to find seats, and Faith sat there in a daze. While it was true that Mr. Anderson had been a complete stranger, they had exchanged letters and had kept each other in their thoughts and prayers. They had planned a future together. Faith sighed; he sounded like he had been a good man. She would have to ask around and find people who knew him. She would like to hear stories about Mr. Jaan Anderson.

Hope was looking around for her sisters. She spotted them sitting in one of the pews and waved, looking puzzled.

"She's probably wondering why she's the only one standing at the altar," Charity whispered to Faith. She waved back and smiled at her sister encouragingly. One by one, Pastor Gregory married the couples in a very basic ceremony, having them recite vows to one another, place rings on their fingers, and kiss. Soon enough, it was Hope's turn.

"Look at little Grace," Charity whispered.

The child was standing beside her father, wearing a flowered yellow dress. She fidgeted and tugged at the waistband of her dress, as if she'd rather have her overalls on, but she settled down to watch her father marry her new stepmother and seemed happy enough about that. After the minister pronounced them man and wife and Hope and Noble had kissed, little Grace tugged at Hope's skirt until she leaned down, whereupon Grace gave her a kiss on the cheek. The three of them happily headed down the aisle and out of the church.

Faith and Charity smiled at one another and then walked outside and joined them.

"Congratulations, Hope," Charity said, bussing her sister on the cheek. She offered her hand to Mr. Enders as Hope introduced him to her sisters.

"Where is Mr. Anders—" Hope began, but before she could finish the question Charity was shaking her head, pulling Hope and her husband aside.

Faith overhead Charity whispering about the loss of Mr. Anderson and also that she herself had refused Mr. Miller.

"I tried to reimburse him for his train ticket," Charity finished.

Hope's eyes grew large. "You refused him?" she asked. "Whatever for? He looked like a good man."

Mr. Enders quickly grasped the enormity of the situation. He took his hat in his hand and said, "As my wife's sisters, I insist that you both come and stay with us at the ranch. We have plenty of room. It's important for family to stick together, especially during difficult times."

Faith's heart warmed as she realized that Hope truly had married a good man.

Charity refused, saying, "Thank you, Mr. Enders, but I think it would be best for us to be in town for the time being. We have a lot to sort out and need to be near Mrs. Reynolds."

"Very well," Mr. Enders said, nodding. "I understand. But as the man in this family, I am taking responsibility for you girls now. I will allow you to remain in town until the first frost, then you will settle in with us for the winter. Promise me you won't take any major steps without consulting me. And I expect both of you to come home with us after church each Sunday for supper."

"Yes, sir," the girls said in unison. Faith and Charity smiled at each other in silent agreement that it was nice to have a man in the family once again.

Music started playing again as the last of the bridal couples left the church. The crowd of people oohed and aahed as a large cake was produced and set on a table in front of the church. Everybody crowded in around it, and a photographer took pictures. Then someone cut the cake and the festivities began. There was music and dancing and someone recited a romantic soliloquy from Shakespeare. Faith looked around; all the brides looked as disoriented and exhausted as she felt, and they each had a marital night ahead of them. Faith, however, would be spending the night, and many more nights to come, in the boarding house with Mrs. Reynolds. And Charity, too, she remembered, glad that she would have one of her sisters with her.

"What are you looking for?" she asked Charity, who kept scanning the crowd.

"Our new little niece, Grace. I want to introduce myself. But she is off running with a group of children."

Faith looked where Charity was pointing, and they both laughed to see the dignified Mr. Enders chasing after his active little daughter.

When the festivities ended, they gathered at the roadside and watched as the brides and their spouses began to disperse. Some left by horse and buggy. Helga and her husband walked down the street hand in hand. Dobie helped Doreen up onto the back of his horse. She held on to him tightly as they rode off, shrieking with laughter.

Mr. Enders helped Hope and little Grace into a horse-drawn buggy. He repeated his offer to house his wife's sisters at his ranch, insisting that his home was theirs, as well.

Charity thanked him profusely and said that perhaps they would take him up on that offer at a later date.

"Come winter, if you girls are still single, I expect you to take up residence with us," he said, looking worried. As they climbed into the buggy, Noble called out, "If either of you should need anything —anything at all—come to me."

They reassured him they would and stood waving as the buggy began to move. Hope tossed something to Charity. For a wild moment, Faith thought it might have been a floral bouquet, but instead, it was her left boot, the one that had the money sealed into the sole. Charity held it over her head and winked knowingly at Hope then joined Faith in waving goodbye.

"I can't believe it. Of the three of us, it's Hope who now has a husband and family," said Faith.

"Yes, sister, besides having a protective brother-in-law, we now have a new little niece. And I'm sure she'll give Hope a run for her money," Charity said, laughing.

The sisters went looking for Mrs. Reynolds so that she could lead them to the boarding house. They soon found her and, as they started walking, she began to scold.

"Charity, Mr. Miller tells me that you refused him. Why would you do that? He was the only man I've met who mentioned being a supporter of the arts. And even though he's a bit older, he's a very good catch, I can assure you. Any number of young women would love to have been matched with him. Now, he has to wait an entire year before I return with a fresh crop of brides."

"I'm too exhausted to discuss it tonight, Mrs. Reynolds," Charity said, although to Faith's eyes she looked as fresh as a daisy. "Please, can this wait until tomorrow?"

"Of course, Charity, but believe me, we will be discussing this," Mrs. Reynolds replied.

The boarding house turned out to be a large white clapboard house near the train station. There were flowers blooming in the front yard and a large garden was visible behind the house. They met their landlady, a heavyset, white-haired woman named Mrs. Barnes.

"Please, girls, make yourselves right at home. I keep an immaculate home, and breakfast and dinner are included in your rent." She gave the girls side by side rooms at the top of the stairs. Mrs. Reynolds had a large apartment on the second story.

And so Faith and Charity settled in at the boarding house, ready to begin the rest of their lives.

CHAPTER 5

*F*aith slept through her first few days in Cheyenne. The heat, she was unaccustomed to, the loss of Mr. Anderson and the long train journey all caught up with her, and for three days, she barely lifted her head from the pillow. Charity roused her and brought her food and drink, which Faith would partake of and go right back to sleep. But finally, the day of reckoning came. Faith awoke and realized that it was time to rejoin the living.

She sat up in bed, stretched her arms, and looked toward the window at the curtains fluttering in the breeze. Today, would be the true beginning of her new life in Cheyenne, Wyoming. She could hear voices. It sounded like Charity arguing with someone. She washed and dressed and then headed downstairs. She passed Charity and Mrs. Reynolds in the parlor. Mrs. Reynolds was scolding her for refusing Mr. Miller, Charity looking as unconcerned as it was possible to be. Next, she wandered into the kitchen, where she found Mrs. Barnes.

"Good morning, young lady. I thought you'd never get out of that bed. Are you feeling better, dear? You've missed out on breakfast, but I have coffee and can make you some eggs, if you'd like."

Faith eyes grew large at a plate of leftover biscuits sitting on the counter. "If you don't mind, these will do just fine, Mrs. Barnes, thank you." She grabbed one and settled down, eating it with the coffee the landlady set before her. She watched as Mrs. Barnes kneaded dough.

"Are you making pie?" Faith asked.

"No, dear, I'm baking bread," Mrs. Barnes said. "Although I'd much rather be out working in my garden, especially on a nice day like this."

"Where is Mr. Barnes?" Faith asked.

"I am a widow," Mrs. Barnes said, wiping away perspiration as she toiled.

"Oh, forgive me, I'm so sorry for your loss," Faith said, feeling terrible for having asked.

"It happened many years ago, dear. Luckily, I had this big house near the train station, so it seemed like a natural thing to do to take in boarders. I like the activity in the house, and it keeps me busy."

"It must be a comfort to you," Faith murmured. "I'm a widow, too, in a way. My intended perished before I reached Wyoming."

Mrs. Barnes clucked sympathetically and brought Faith a slice of ham to eat.

"Mrs. Barnes, I wanted to tell you that I love to bake, my specialty being pies. Do you think it would be possible for me to make one once in a while?"

"Anytime you'd like to bake anything at all, you go right ahead," Mrs. Barnes assured her. "As long as you make extra to serve to the boarders for dessert."

Just then, Charity entered the kitchen.

"Are you all right?" Faith asked, wondering if Charity had gotten her feelings hurt when Mrs. Reynolds scolded her.

"Perfectly all right. As I told Mrs. Reynolds, I know exactly what I'm doing." Charity told Mrs. Barnes that she didn't care for any coffee as she'd had a cup at breakfast. "You're both right. There was nothing wrong with Mr. Slade Miller, but I'm just now beginning to deal with losing Thomas. I find it's helping to be away from Boston and all the memories it held of us together there," Charity sadly shared. "As soon as I looked at Mr. Miller, I knew it was just too soon to enter into another relationship."

Faith patted her sister's arm. Charity wasn't being dramatic, for a change. Instead, she was confiding in her sister about her pain over the breakup of her engagement.

Suddenly, Charity smiled at Faith and pulled a brown velvet purse out of her waistband. "Faith, do you remember what this is?" she asked.

Faith looked puzzled for a moment and then gasped, recalling the banker holding out the bag. "It's Mr. Anderson's life savings," she said sorrowfully.

"Shall we pour it out and count it?" Charity asked.

"No, no," Faith said, leaning back. "I can't accept it; really, I can't. It belongs to his next of kin, or perhaps it should be donated to his favorite charity."

"Nonsense!" said Mrs. Barnes, joining them at the table.

"I beg your pardon?" Faith asked. She had forgotten the landlady was nearby.

"I'm sorry for eavesdropping, girls, but I knew Mr. Jaan Anderson. I knew him very well, in fact. You see, I am his next of kin as he was my younger brother."

Tears sprang to Faith's eyes. "Oh, I had no idea, I'm so sorry," she said, but Mrs. Barnes took the pouch from Charity and poured the contents out onto the kitchen table.

"I insist that you keep this money, Faith. I told the banker that it should go to the young woman who had left her life behind and traveled all this way expecting to have a husband welcoming her. I knew that you would have unexpected expenses. As you can see, dear, there is plenty here to last you for a long while. And now that

I can see what a good-hearted person you are, I definitely want you to have it."

"But, Mrs. Barnes, oh, I just don't know."

"I insist, dear. As you can see, I am very comfortable with my income from taking in boarders. And even though you and Jaan never wed, I hope you, both of you, will still think of me as family. Do you think you could do that?"

Faith was too overcome to reply, but Charity spoke for her. She thanked the landlady warmly, adding that, "It's wonderful to have family here in Wyoming."

Faith finally found her voice. "Please, tell me all about Mr. Anderson. I want to know what he was like."

"There will be plenty of time for that later," Mrs. Barnes replied. "An entire lifetime, in fact. Faith, finish your breakfast, and then, Charity, why don't you take your sister out for a walk? It's a beautiful day. Go do a little exploring. We have a very fine needlework shop just down the street. Also, you must stop in at the mercantile."

After eating, Faith freshened up and joined Charity for a walk down Main street. Mrs. Barnes had given them a basket, in case they made any purchases. They easily found the needlework shop. Apparently, there were a lot of sheep in Wyoming, as there was a dazzling display of yarn in bright cheerful colors. Faith handled some of them. A group of women were sitting at a table knitting. The shop owner suggested that Faith and Charity come back and knit with the women one day.

"Knit? I'll be far too busy for that," said Charity as Faith thanked the lady for asking. "Busy doing what?" Faith asked as they exited the store and set off down the street.

"Whatever it takes to start a theater, of course. Then I'll be busy forming a theater company."

"Don't you think you're putting the cart before the horse?" Faith asked.

"I don't understand," Charity said.

"Shouldn't you be putting your life together, first?" Faith replied. "Finding a husband, building a future. Shouldn't founding a theater come after all that?"

"I don't think you understand how important theater is to me, and not just to me but to the universe," Charity cried. "I've asked around, and there isn't a theater west of the Mississippi. If I'm going to marry, it will be someone I meet through my theatrical pursuits."

Faith sighed. She turned away and then spotted a grey, two-story building across the street and down the block. *Miller Mercantile,* the letters above the shop said.

"There it is," she said hopefully to Charity.

Charity looked where Faith was pointing and stared blankly at the store.

"Perhaps it isn't too late, Charity. Go talk to Mr. Miller, explain that you were exhausted from the journey and you've reconsidered."

Charity began to flush as her anger built. "I am not marrying some old man, Faith. Get that through your head."

"Pardon me, but I thought he was very nice looking and not all that old."

"Then you marry him," Charity snapped, turning and walking away.

Faith called to Charity to come back, but her sister turned a corner and was soon out of sight. It was too nice a day to go back home, and she felt unusually brave. She could see the boarding house when she turned around, so it gave her the courage to keep moving forward. She headed towards the mercantile. Mrs. Reynolds had said it was quite impressive and she hadn't been exaggerating. Faith walked further, then she saw something that made her stop dead in her tracks. A group of women were standing in front of a shop window chatting gaily. One of them pointed something out to the others, and they all began to laugh. Out loud, on the street—an unthinkable breach of etiquette in Boston.

But Faith was no longer in Boston. She was in sunny Wyoming, where it seemed perfectly natural to see people enjoying themselves out in public. A gentleman passed her by, a complete stranger. He smiled and tipped his hat at her. Faith blushed at getting unexpected male attention. When it happened three more times during her two-minute walk, she began to gain confidence. She broke out into a smile and began to swing her basket as she walked, humming a little tune. To her surprise, she found that she was not as homesick for Boston as she thought she would be. Being near her sisters made her feel that she had brought home along with her.

Faith looked around, pleased. Cheyenne was much larger than she had envisioned. She had expected clapboard walkways atop dusty roads, but the roads were lined in stones and the walkways clearly laid out.

She passed the blacksmith shop and peeked inside. She could hear the bellows and saw a large, muscular man wearing a black apron and pounding on a horseshoe. He looked up at her and smiled, his white teeth contrasting with his dark skin. She smiled back shyly and hurried away.

She turned a corner and collided with a tall gentleman wearing a Stetson. The collision caused her to fall backwards and drop her basket. She was caught by a strong pair of arms who pulled her upright. At first, she thought it must be one of the cowboys that this new land had in such plentiful supply, but when she looked up, she found herself looking into a pair of concerned blue eyes.

They stood frozen in time, the two of them; he was holding her shoulders as he asked if she was okay. The person whom she'd collided with, who was now seemingly reluctant to let go of her, was Mr. Slade Miller, Charity's ex-fiancé and owner of the mercantile.

Faith looked up into his handsome face, and for a wild moment, thought that he was going to lean forward to kiss her. Instead, the gentleman seemed to come back to himself. Once he made certain that Faith was once again steady on her feet, he bent over and picked up the basket she'd dropped.

"Pardon me, ma'am," he said, tipping his hat to her and handing her back the basket. Their hands touched, and a shiver went up Faith's spine.

"Thank you, Mr. Miller," Faith said, lowering her eyes. Her heart was beating so hard, she almost couldn't catch her breath. It took her a long moment to compose herself. The man before her was one of the handsomest she'd ever seen. He, too, seemed affected by their explosive first meeting, stepping back and taking in the sight of her. He did not, however, seem at all surprised to find that a stranger knew his name. Faith supposed that owning the biggest store in town would make a person recognizable to all.

"Are you all right, miss? And where are you heading, if I may be so bold?" Mr. Miller asked.

"To the mercantile."

"What a coincidence. That's where I'm heading. Let me escort you," he said, taking her elbow and steering her towards his store. "I'm afraid you have me at a disadvantage, miss, for you know my name but I do not have the pleasure of knowing yours. I don't believe I have ever seen you before. You would not have happened to arrive in town on the bride train, would you?"

Faith's heart dropped. She would have to tell this man her name. As soon as he discovered that she was related to the woman who had broken his heart, he would certainly have a much different reaction than the electrified exchange they had just shared on the street corner. She stood back as her escort opened the door to the store and gestured for her to lead the way. Faith stepped over the threshold and then turned, watching Mr. Miller close the door behind him and adjust the bell that rang whenever anyone entered. He had a square, strong jaw, a full head of brown hair, parted in the middle and swept back, and the skin around his eyes crinkled when he smiled. The thought occurred to Faith that he had a face she would not mind looking upon for the rest of her days. She reluctantly identified herself.

"My name is Faith, Mr. Miller. Faith Cummings."

"Cummings?" he asked, his handsome face contorting into a scowl. "You would not happen to be related to Miss Charity Cummings?"

"Yes, sir, Charity is my little sister."

"I'm sorry to hear that," he said, drawing himself up to his full height and walking away from her to take his place behind the counter. She watched him greet his co-worker and then don a dark blue apron. His manner towards her became a stark contrast to the warmth with which he had initially spoken to her.

"Please, Mr. Miller, I hope you won't hold that against me," Faith said, rushing to the counter. "Charity is, well, she is very young and suffering from a broken engagement. She just needs time to heal and doesn't yet know her own heart. I can assure you that her actions were not wise nor well thought out. You mustn't take her rejection personally."

Mr. Miller, whose name tag said *Slade* turned from her and became busy arranging spices on the shelf behind him. He had undoubtedly been greatly shamed by Charity's refusal. What was wrong with that sister of hers? Faith thought, not for the first time. There was certainly nothing wrong with Mr. Miller. He stood tall and incredibly handsome; what more could any woman want? But Charity, as usual, had other ideas about her future, strange ideas which involved bringing theater to the Great Plains. Mr. Miller began to greet customers and appeared much too busy to continue to converse with Faith.

She decided then and there that she would gift Mr. Miller with one of her famous pies. It would in no way make up for the loss of her beautiful sister, but perhaps it would move him to think kindly of the Cummings girls. She walked around the store, choosing peaches and sugar, flour and shortening. She put her selections in her basket then tentatively walked to the counter and set her basket upon it, waiting to be helped. It was not Mr. Miller who came to count up her purchases but rather his assistant, a thin, wiry older man whose name badge declared that he was *Nate*.

"That will be eight cents, miss," he said, holding out his hand. Faith paid him and turned to walk out of the store. She looked back sorrowfully over her shoulder at Mr. Miller. He was now helping an elderly matron choose fabric. He did not look at her nor wish her goodbye, as most shopkeepers would have done. It was Nate who called out, "Good day."

Sadly, Faith exited the mercantile and began to walk back to the boarding house. She felt bad that there was already someone in Cheyenne who did not like them. She would have to warn Hope not to use her maiden name around Mr. Miller. Faith chuckled as she thought about how Hope had been the sister most reluctant to enter into a mail order bride arrangement and yet she was the only one who was now married and settled. Faith reached the boarding house and found their landlady, Mrs. Barnes, cutting roses in the garden. She greeted her warmly.

"Hello there, dearie," Mrs. Barnes called out. "I've tidied up the kitchen for you in the hopes that you might return with some pie-baking ingredients. Feel free to use anything you need."

"Thank you, Mrs. Barnes, it's going to be peach pie tonight." Mrs. Barnes smiled and Faith headed right to the kitchen. She set her purchases out on the counter and got to work, preparing the dough and rolling it out. She settled happily into her familiar routine, letting her mind wander as she peeled and sliced the peaches.

Before it seemed humanly possible, Faith had three large peach pies cooling on the window sill. She had found the spacious boarding house kitchen to be even easier to work in than the little kitchen she'd had in Boston.

"If those pies taste as good as they smell, I predict you will have quite an industry for yourself here in Wyoming," Mrs. Barnes said as she entered the kitchen with a basket full of freshly picked roses.

"What do you mean?" Faith asked.

"There are several places in town that serve dessert, and a good baker is always in demand."

"I once thought about making pies for a living, but I feared it would not pay more than pocket money," Faith said.

"It all depends on how you go about it," Mrs. Barnes replied cryptically. Before Faith could question her further, both Mrs. Reynolds and Charity entered the kitchen. Faith had resolved to avoid the matchmaker, not wanting to be matched with anyone yet. The matchmaker began fluttering around the two girls in a motherly fashion.

"How good to see you up and about, Faith," Mrs. Reynolds said. Charity kissed Faith on the cheek and sat across from her as Mrs. Barnes busied herself making a pot of coffee.

"Charity, where did you go? What are you up to?" Faith asked.

"I went to look for vacant buildings, of course. Do you think it's easy to build a theater from scratch?" Charity asked, as if the answer were obvious."

"Don't you think you should put first things first, dear?" Mrs. Reynolds asked kindly. "You need to focus your attention on finding a wealthy husband who can finance such a venture. I've had a lot of inquiries about you, Charity."

"That's exactly what I told her, Mrs. Reynolds," Faith said, glaring at her sister.

"Absolutely not, Mrs. Reynolds," Charity replied with a tone bordering on disrespect. "A husband will want me barefoot and pregnant and resent my passion for the theater. I'll not marry until I'm good and ready. Why, I may not wed until my thirties, if at all."

All three women gasped at this.

"I still don't see what was wrong with Mr. Miller," Faith said. "You know, he's quite upset with all of us. And he is the local shopkeeper. He is perfectly good looking and would treat his wife well."

"As I said, you marry him, then," Charity retorted with a toss of her curls.

"He wants nothing to do with any of us," Faith said sorrowfully.

"I would like to show you girls some pictures of the local men who might be interested," Mrs. Reynolds said, pressing on. "I know that you two probably think you don't need my services at this point, since the town is crawling with men looking for wives, but please consider that I know, or know of, most of the single men in this town and I can advise you on whether a certain gentleman is all that he is presenting himself to be. If I do not know him, I have the connections to make discreet inquiries."

"The dream of moving west certainly attracts some colorful characters," Mrs. Barnes agreed. "I'm sure two pretty girls like you are turning more than your share of heads, but listen to Mrs. Reynolds. This is the biggest step of your life; don't leave things to chance if you don't have to."

"My pie!" Faith said, leaping to her feet. She had intended to deliver one of the pies to Mr. Miller while it was still warm. She wrapped the best-looking pie in a dishcloth, placed it in her basket, and then rushed out of the house. She was back a moment later, unpinning her apron, then rushed out again.

"What was that about?" Charity asked, watching her sister bustle out the door.

"I have no idea," Mrs. Barnes said.

Mrs. Reynolds watched Faith go, one eyebrow raised. What indeed was that about? What on earth would make shy, timid, matronly Faith behave like a young girl? She frowned, turning back to Charity and making her look at pictures of the wealthier men in town.

CHAPTER 6

*F*aith slipped into the mercantile. She didn't see Mr. Miller, but Nate greeted her warmly. She set her basket on the counter and removed the pie.

Nate gave an appreciate sniff. "Do you want us to sell that for you, miss? It would bring a good price."

"No," Faith said, shaking her head. "This is a gift for Mr. Miller. Tell him that, well, tell him it is my hope he won't think too badly of our family."

"Tell him, yourself," Nate said, smiling and looking behind her. Faith turned around to see Mr. Miller walking toward her.

"Tell me what?" he asked.

Once again, Faith found her breath taken away by the good-looking shopkeeper. She composed herself and delivered the speech she had practiced on the way over.

"Mr. Miller, I baked you a pie. I know it won't make up for the loss of Charity, but it's my sincere hope that you won't hold the actions of an eighteen-year-old girl against the rest of us."

Mr. Miller smiled, but his eyes were cold. There were other people in the shop, so Faith assumed he had spoken to her so as not to appear rude. She took the dishcloth off the pie and scurried out of the shop.

As Faith got back to the boarding house, she passed a gentleman emerging from the parlor. He gave Faith an appreciative look as he headed out the door. He was tall, slender, and fair, with pale blond hair.

"Who was that?" she asked Mrs. Reynolds, who was emerging from the parlor.

"That is Mr. Bernard Olsen. He owns the dairy farm next to Noble's ranch."

"You don't say," said Faith. "Right next to Noble and Hope?"

"Yes, and he's very impressed with Hope. He has seen how well she's settled into life in Wyoming and has just commissioned me to find him a wife."

"Really?" Faith said. "He lives right next to Hope?" she asked again.

"Yes, Faith, and the gentleman has two boys who are about to turn twenty. You might consider him. His dairy farm is very successful. It supplies milk for the entire state."

"There you are," Mrs. Barnes said as she and Mrs. Reynolds headed into the kitchen.

"Faith dear, I know that it's a little early, but some very nice gentlemen have come forward to ask about you," Mrs. Reynolds went on, indifferent to Mrs. Barnes presence. "There are still all the men in my book plus a crop of fresh ones, like Mr. Olsen, who are coming to see me daily. Could I at least run some of them past you?"

"Bernard Olsen?" Mrs. Barnes asked, overhearing the end of the conversation.

Faith sighed and began to apologize to Mrs. Barnes. "I'm so sorry, I had hoped not to discuss anything of this nature in front of you," she said, throwing Mrs. Reynolds an exasperated look.

"Why ever not?" Mrs. Barnes asked, wiping her hands on her apron. "Oh, is it because of Jaan?" When Faith nodded, she said.

"Now, that's just nonsense, Faith. I know you two had written and thought about each other, but you never even met him. And I won't have you putting your life on hold for some arbitrary length of time because you think it's proper. You have to strike while the iron's hot, girl!"

Faith laughed, relieved.

"And Mr. Bernard Olsen is a fine man. He and his parents traveled over on the same boat from Sweden that Jaan and I did. Of course, he was just a boy, and we were adults. I've watched him grow. He built that dairy farm from the ground up and married the prettiest girl in town. It was a terrible thing when his wife died birthing those boys, but he's done a fine job of raising them. You could do much worse, Faith."

"See, darling girl, Mrs. Barnes understands that you aren't getting any younger. Trust me, dear, it's much better to quickly state your intentions toward one man in particular than to wander around town unencumbered. There is such a shortage of women that it could quickly turn into a bull fight."

"Mrs. Reynolds!" Faith said, shocked. "You are referring to gentlemen, not animals. I'm sure that everyone will conduct themselves appropriately, even if I were to have more than one suitor."

Mrs. Reynolds sighed loudly. "Faith, you aren't in Boston anymore. This is the west, and a lot of men here have been without female company for quite some time. And it's the men with the least to lose who are the most aggressive. Do you understand what I'm saying?"

Faith nodded; she couldn't argue with reasoning like that. Mrs. Reynolds certainly knew Cheyenne better than she did. "All right, who do you have in mind?"

This made Mrs. Reynolds happy and she reached into her pocket and produced a handful of photographs. All three women gathered around the kitchen table to look at them.

"Now you don't have to rush into anything, Faith dear. But these gentlemen would certainly appreciate permission to come calling. What could it hurt to spend a little time getting to know them? Even if you don't marry one of them, think of it as meeting people in your new community."

"All right," Faith said reluctantly. "But it seems to me that this is just stirring up trouble."

Mrs. Reynolds set a picture down and slid it across the table to Faith.

"Pastor Gregory!" Faith said. "Are you serious? He's single?"

"His wife died a few years back. He's raising four children with the help of an elderly aunt. It isn't easy."

"He's not very good looking, is he?" Faith asked doubtfully. The pastor was balding but slender. "And four children? My goodness. I'm not certain—"

"I know that, Faith, but he is a man of God."

"Most women would be proud to be the pastor's wife," Mrs. Barnes pointed out.

"What is his first name?" Faith asked.

"Godwin," Mrs. Reynolds replied.

"Godwin Gregory, are you serious?" she asked.

"Yes, he's of Scottish descent," Mrs. Barnes replied. Faith looked at the two of them. They seemed to know a great deal about everyone in town.

"Pastor Gregory was with the group of men at the train station who informed me about Jaan's passing," Faith reminisced. "As I recall, he's not very tall," she said. "How old is he?"

"Younger than you'd think. His hair is thinning, which makes him appear older. He's just thirty-three."

"I'll take a good look at him at church on Sunday and let you know what I think."

"Here's another one," Mrs. Reynolds's said, handing her another photograph.

Faith knew she had never seen this gentleman before. He had a moustache and an ethnic look to him.

"He's nice looking," said Faith. "What's his name?"

"Mario Martinelli, he immigrated here from Italy. He has family here in Cheyenne. It could be good for you to be embraced by a large Italian family."

Faith nodded slowly, contemplating the idea.

"He's opening an Italian restaurant in town. You could make the desserts."

Faith shrugged and handed the picture back to Mrs. Reynolds.

"There are many more, dear. Let's go through that book of mine sometime."

"All right, Mrs. Reynolds. I'll look for these gentlemen at church on Sunday and then give you my final decision," Faith said.

The next day was Sunday, and Faith was up and dressed and in Charity's room, hurrying her along.

"I'm not sure I even want to go to church," said Charity, fluffing up her hair.

"You cause enough gossip and speculation without failing to be seen at church, young lady. You are definitely accompanying me. Besides, we'll get to see Hope. Say, did you ever get the money out of her shoe?"

"No, then we'd just have to hide it. It's already well hidden. No one would steal a single old boot that's in the bottom of an armoire under some dirty laundry. Let's leave it put until we need it."

"Well, we'll have to see how Hope feels about that," Faith said. She hurried Charity out the door before she even had time to tie her bonnet in place. They were one of the first to arrive at church. They stood outside the entrance, watching people arrive.

"I'm surprised," said Charity.

"By what?" Faith asked.

"The women's' clothing is really very stylish. There are some homespun exceptions but, by and large, everyone looks well turned out."

Faith looked around, surprised. She never noticed things like that, but it was true. The townspeople could have been in Boston, so well turned out were they. Faith and Charity spotted Helga and her besotted husband. Doreen came running up with Dobie close behind, both of them beaming with happiness. Faith saw the Spanish sisters walking hand in hand with their husbands. Bespectacled Edith, the former school marm, was staring up at her handsome cowboy husband with a look of awe. Faith and Charity were drawing several curious stares. Soon, there were a half a dozen men standing around them. Charity was talking with a young man whom Faith didn't know, chatting away as if she'd known him all her life. Faith sighed and stared at the ground, hoping that no one would speak to her.

"Hello there, Miss Cummings," she heard and looked up to see Slade Miller looking down at her. "I haven't had a chance to speak to you since you dropped off that pie."

Faith felt her heart swell in her chest. She blushed, being unaccustomed to such a feeling. She looked around and saw that Charity was standing about fifteen feet away with her back to the two of them, still talking to the same young man.

"I hope you liked it," she said, her voice trailing off into a whisper.

"I liked it just fine. Nate and I ate the whole thing, that very afternoon. I didn't even get a chance to take any of it home."

"I'm so glad, Mr. Miller." The chimes rang to enter church, so Faith was spared from having to make further small talk. She led Charity up to the front of the church, hoping Mr. Miller would sit nowhere nearby. She wanted to keep her sister away from the shop owner, afraid that he was still very angry with her.

Hope arrived shortly afterward and led her little family into the pew beside her sisters. Faith was surprised by how her sister looked. Hope seemed younger and prettier, her eyes sparkling in a new way. She had the front and sides of her hair up but had let the back hang down.

"Your hair is down!" Faith whispered to her, shocked.

"We're not in Boston anymore, sister," Hope replied, tossing her hair the same way Charity usually did.

"How are you?" Charity asked.

"I'm fine, how are you two?" she whispered back, but Pastor Gregory was approaching the altar, signaling that the service was to begin. Faith watched him carefully. He was not especially attractive but did appear to be younger than one would think, at first. He had kind eyes. She looked around to see who his four children might be and spotted them sitting in the front row, three girls and a delicate little boy, sitting with an elderly woman who must have been the pastor's aunt. She then spotted Mario Martinelli. He was very swarthy and dark, short and wide. He had a wide smile and a playful manner. Every time Faith turned to peek at him, he was smiling. He had a woman at his side who resembled him, perhaps a sister?

She did not see Bernard Olsen until the congregation approached the altar for communion, one by one. She saw him with his two sons; he appeared to be somewhat stern and serious. Mrs. Reynolds had presented her with an intriguing assortment of men, that much was for certain. On their way back to their seats, he gave her a nod. She knew he was interested. Faith sat back, imagining living just a hop, skip, and a jump away from Hope and Noble.

After church, the girls filed out and stood outside talking. Mr. Enders was keeping an eye on Grace, who was chasing after other children.

"So, how is married life?" Charity asked with a twinkle in her eye.

"Well, I haven't found anything not to like yet," Hope said in that blunt way of hers. "Did you get the money out of my shoe?"

"No, not yet. None of us need it yet, so I thought it was safest being in some old boot tossed in my armoire.

"No," said Hope. "Take it to the shoe repair and have them remove the sole in a way that none of the paper money is damaged.

Then have him repair the shoe. Count the money right in front of him. There should be six hundred dollars there."

"Do you need the money immediately?" Faith asked, concerned.

"No but we will need some of it when that Homestead Act passes. How are you two doing for money?

Both Faith and Charity assured Hope they were doing fine.

"I mean it, count that money when he's removing it from the shoe. I don't trust anyone, even the shoe repair in Boston. I watched him seal the money inside the boot, but I want to make sure he didn't pull some slight of hand. Make sure it's all there."

"What should I do with it once I have it in hand?" asked Charity.

"Go to the bank and put it in a compound interest earning account in all three of our names. That way, all three of us will need to be present to withdraw it. And when we stake our claim, the land will be in all three of our names."

The three girls were set upon by some single gentlemen. Faith ended up chatting with all three of the men whom Mrs. Reynolds had attempted to match her with. Her first impressions seemed to be spot on. Mario was cheerful and playful, Bernard serious and watchful. Pastor Gregory chatted with all three girls, welcoming them to the church and inviting them to Wednesday night Bible study. Mario and Bernard each asked Faith if they could come calling. Faith became very uncomfortable at this and didn't know what to say, so she ended up nodding in agreement to them both. She hadn't wanted to make snap judgments but felt concerned that it would appear unseemly to be entertaining more than one gentlemen caller. But she was in a boarding house, she remembered. Nobody would think anything of men coming and going from such a place.

Just then, Mr. Enders pulled up with his horse-drawn buggy, and the three girls and Grace climbed in.

"I can't wait to show you girls around the ranch," Mr. Enders said as he spurred the horses into motion. Faith murmured a polite response, but Charity was in the back of the buggy playing a hand clapping game with Grace. The ranch was not that far out; it only took a half hour or so to get there. Faith looked out over the landscape that she had only seen before from the train window. It was beautiful country; there was no doubt about it, with rolling green hills, mountains in the background, and various settlements dotting the horizon.

Mr. Enders clucked at the horses, pulling on the reins as they pulled up to a wooden gate. Hope hopped out of the buggy and opened the gate, which had an iron arch at the top proclaiming it to be the *Triple E Ranch*. As they rolled in the gate, Faith gasped at how immense the property appeared to be.

"Triple E?" she asked Mr. Enders.

"The ranch was founded by my father. There was my father, my mother, and myself, and so, Triple E," he explained.

"There's the main house, and that's the barn," Hope said, pointing out the various buildings.

Charity asked, "What were all those small buildings on the ranch?"

"Outhouses, quarters for the ranch hands, a smoke house, and the silo over there stores grain," Hope replied, pointing to the various buildings.

The ranch was beautiful, Faith thought, set back on acres of green land. She could see horses and cows grazing. It gave her a queer feeling in the pit of her stomach, though, to imagine her sister living in such a place. There had always just been the three of them in their little brownstone in Boston.

Hope laughed at Faith's dazed expression as she looked around. "Wonderful, isn't it? I love the wide-open spaces," she said.

Faith agreed that it was quite impressive.

"And your sister has been a Godsend," Mr. Enders added, smiling over at Hope. "We sure do enjoy her cooking and baking, don't we, Grace?" he added, calling back over his shoulder to his daughter.

"Yup, Papa, good food," agreed Grace as the three sisters laughed.

Faith was surprised to hear him praise Hope's cooking and baking. She knew her sister to be a reluctant cook, at best. Mr. Enders let them off outside the house, and Hope led her sisters and little Grace inside.

"Grace, get that dog out of here!" Hope called.

Grace tugged a big, hairy beast, the one in Mrs. Reynolds photograph, outside.

Charity followed, chuckling at the little girl's pluck.

"Oh dear, the animal looks so fierce. Are you sure it's safe for Grace to be handling him?" Faith asked.

"That little girl is a wonder with animals. I wouldn't hesitate to trust her with a wild stallion," said Hope proudly.

Faith smiled at Hope. She had embraced little Grace as her own, she could tell. As Hope took off her wrap and deftly donned an apron, Faith wandered around the kitchen in wonder. It was large and well stocked. On a side table, she saw a bulge under a dishcloth and lifted it to discover a very tall cake. It had white frosting and strawberries on top.

"Did you make this?" Faith asked as she donned an extra apron hanging from a post.

"Yep, I sure did. I find that I enjoy cooking for a hungry family. You were right, Faith, we do feed the ranch hands, Hank, Nelson and Bertha, quite often, in fact. Others come by to help at various times, depending on what's happening. Bertha is the ranch foreman; you have to meet her. She wears men's trousers and can trick ride and shoot. She's even teaching me to shoot. She says I have a natural ability. I truly think that good eyesight is half of it, and the other half is a steady hand."

"Yes, I'd like to meet a woman like that," Faith said, although she wasn't so sure that was true. A woman who shot and rode and wore trousers? What next? "You are learning to shoot a gun?" she asked, stunned.

"A rifle, a person's got to be able to defend what's theirs in this country," Hope replied, patting down some biscuits.

"In case of Indians?" Faith asked fearfully.

"No we don't have problems with the Indians in these parts. Noble's mother was a Cherokee."

"Noble—" Faith gasped.

Before she could go on, Hope threw her a look. "His dad arrived from Europe. There weren't a lot of women around, and he ended up marrying an Indian princess.

"Why wouldn't Mrs. Reynolds have informed us of that?" Faith whispered, shocked.

"She did tell me about it when you were making more tea. I was fine with it. I feel alive here, Faith, like my life in Boston was just a dream from a distant past. There's a lot of work, it's true, but I'm more than up to the challenge. It energizes me. Noble told me how things are done around here. Monday is laundry day, Tuesday is for baking, and on it goes. I am planning to keep to the schedule, for the time being."

"And Mr. Enders, do you feel comfortable with him?" Faith asked.

"I most certainly do. You've talked to him; he's such a good man, Faith. I like him and, in time, I'm sure I'll come to love him. Maybe I already do," she said, stopping what she was doing and looking off in the distance.

"Well, thank goodness then that you'll give up this homesteading idea."

"Says who?" Hope replied. "I plan to get my own land and work it myself, I've decided. I'll let you and Charity, Grace and Bertha help me, but none of the men. I want to prove we women can do our own homesteading."

"What does Mr. Enders think of all this?" Faith asked with concern.

"He said he'd be right proud to have a woman with her own

land," Hope replied. "He wants little Grace to learn to be self-sufficient," she added.

"How unusual," Faith murmured, but she supposed that was how men thought, here in the wild west.

"And what about you, Faith? What have you been up to?"

Faith had taken a knife and was cutting some fruit. She shook her head, trying not to dwell on the fact that "I spent the first few days here in bed. I don't know what it was, but I just felt so overwhelmed and exhausted. Our landlady, Mrs. Barnes, is Jaan Anderson's sister. Isn't that an amazing coincidence?" Faith asked.

"Not really, the Great Plains are being settled by families, large ones," Hope replied.

"She's letting me bake pies in her kitchen. I can tell she hates baking, so I'm planning to take it over, bit by bit. Monday, I'll make biscuits, Tuesday, breads, and so forth. She said my pies are so good that I might be able to sell them around town."

"I have no doubt that's true, Faith. Folks are very busy here and would pay for the convenience."

"And Mrs. Reynolds is trying to match me with some men. Pastor Gregory, Mario, who is opening an Italian restaurant, and a farmer named Bernard Olsen."

"Bernard Olsen, our neighbor? He seems like a fine man," Hope replied.

"Oh, I almost forget, when you go into the mercantile, don't tell the owner your maiden name. He's a little bitter about being refused by Charity," said Faith, changing the subject away from her love life.

"Talking about me?" Charity asked, leading Grace back inside.

"Actually, Faith was telling me about some men Mrs. Reynolds has in mind for her. And you, Charity, what happened after you refused Mr. Miller? Have any other men expressed an interest?"

Charity shrugged. "I don't have time for all that. I'm busy trying to find a vacant building to hold the theater. Did you know there is already a committee in town trying to build an opera house? I'm considering joining them."

"You don't say," Hope replied. "Did you know about all this?" she asked Faith.

"Yes, I hardly see her," Faith said, and Hope looked at her younger sister sharply.

"Well, before you go tromping through vacant buildings by yourself, perhaps you should secure an escort?" Hope scolded.

"What does that mean?" Charity snapped.

"Just because this is the wild west, it doesn't mean that you don't have to still protect your reputation," Hope snapped back.

"Oh, for Heaven's sake. Listen, you two, I am never going to be your typical young lady. Everyone will just have to get used to that. And you, Hope, I thought you'd appreciate that I was spending my time and energy on a project I believe in and not just sitting around the parlor entertaining gentlemen callers."

A little old dark-skinned woman walked into the kitchen and began lifting lids and stirring pots. Faith raised her eyebrow and looked at Hope.

"Girls, this is Maria Tallfeather; she is the housekeeper around here. Maria, these are my sisters, Faith and Charity."

Maria gave them a nod and a smile, then she started setting the table.

"Housekeeper?" Faith asked.

"Yep, this was a working ranch long before I came on the scene. She has practically raised Grace, according to Noble. Come on, girls, let me show you around the place." She turned to Maria and said a few words in a foreign language and then led her sisters out of the kitchen.

"Was that French?" Charity asked Hope.

"No, that was Comanche. I've picked up a few words of it, and Maria knows some English, so we communicate well enough."

"My goodness, Hope. You have really taken the bull by the horns here," said Faith, impressed. "You are cooking and baking and learning a new language. You are a wife and mother. It's all just so ironic."

"I know. I don't think I'd have been as good a wife in a small house in Boston, but ranching life agrees with me."

"Married life suits you, as well," agreed Charity.

Hope showed them around the parlor and the bedrooms.

"Your house is so large," said Faith. "It just goes on and on."

"Noble said it started out as a little log cabin built by his father, but they've added to it over the years. Noble's mother was an Indian, as is Maria," she informed Charity, who'd been outside when Hope had mentioned it earlier.

"You don't say!" said Charity. "That means that little Grace is one-quarter Indian."

"It would explain her straight hair and beautiful brown eyes," mused Faith.

"And her way with animals," Hope added.

Faith's head was spinning. It was all a lot to take in. Oh, Faith knew they would encounter Indians in their new world but hadn't expected to end up related to some.

Hope did not miss Faith's reaction. "Noble is a fine upstanding member of the community, sister," she said, daring Faith to respond in the negative. "I'm happy to be married to such a man."

"I had no idea," Faith murmured.

Her sister was married to an Indian, and if she had children, they would be part Cherokee. She studied Noble through dinner. With his wide brow, brown eyes, and dark hair that swept back off his brow, he truly looked like an Indian. How could she not have spotted it before? She had to admit that she admired his quiet dignity and calm manner.

After dinner, Hope led them into her bedroom, and as they were looking around, Faith spotted something hanging on the wall. It appeared to be a paddle. It had a handle attached to a wooden board. She was shocked into silence as her cheeks grew red. A paddle? Did Mr. Enders spank little Grace? But why was it in the bedroom?"

Charity didn't seem to notice; it blended in with the wood walls behind it. She was chatting away with Hope and commenting on the quilt on the bed.

As they left the room, Faith held back for a moment, studying the paddle. She made a mental note to ask Hope about it later.

Bertha and Hope drove Faith and Charity back home after dinner. Faith couldn't believe how easily the foreman handled the reins and the horses. Faith, Hope and Charity sat in the wagon so they could talk.

"Bertha is going to teach me how to lead the team," Hope informed them.

"I want to ask you about something," Faith said to Hope. "I saw something hanging on the wall in the bedroom. A paddle," she added, her voice trailing off to a whisper.

"Does Mr. Enders paddle little Grace?" Charity asked.

"When Grace has been naughty, Noble takes her out to the woodshed. But the paddle is for me."

"Hope!" Faith and Charity both said in unison.

Hope turned to look at them with as much aplomb as if she'd just announced that she'd hung the wash out to dry.

"Yes, according to Bertha, it's the code of the west. She said the men believe in controlling their livestock, young'uns and womenfolk. Isn't that quaint?"

"You can't mean to say that your husband paddles you?" said Faith, shocked.

"Yup, on the bare bottom, too."

"You've already earned a paddling?" Charity asked, seemingly amused by the entire thing.

"Noble didn't care for the tone of voice I used when talking to the servants. I thought I was being respectful, but let me tell you, after that paddling, I'm very careful about the tone of voice I use. It stung like there was no tomorrow. I was dancing around the room afterward, I can tell you."

Faith put her hand to her flushed cheek. The entire conversation was a little too much for her. To think that if she and Charity chose husbands, they might be put over their knees at some point? She just couldn't envision such a thing. But that night, in bed, Faith lay staring up at the ceiling, feeling strangely stimulated. Oh, yes, she'd been impressed by Hope's ranch and her new family, but it was more than that. She fell asleep thinking about that paddle hanging on the wall, and she couldn't stop thinking about it.

CHAPTER 7

*F*aith bowed her head, studying her Bible. She'd been given the seat of honor in Bible study, at Pastor Gregory's right hand. Faith's mind wasn't on her Bible, though. Instead, she was wondering what a courtship with a man of God would be like. She looked over at Charity, who had a rapt, angelic expression on her face as the words of Jesus were being read by the pastor. Faith was not impressed; her sister always had the perfect expression on her face, no matter what the occasion. Just last Sunday, she had looked worldly and bemused when hearing about Hope's paddling.

Suddenly, Faith's attention was caught by something the pastor was saying. Something about domestic discipline, a term she'd never heard before. The pastor had read a scripture from the Bible, which Faith had not paid attention to, but he went on to explain that the man was dominant and the woman submissive. This, he explained, was pleasing in the eyes of God and had the effect of creating an orderly Christian household.

Hands were raised and questions asked, and a couple of folks even shared stories of how discipline was maintained in their households. Faith's head began to swim. What kind of a world had she landed in? She was quite sure that none of those things happened in Boston. She tried to imagine a church friend of hers, a young woman named Sophia who had married about a year prior. She closed her eyes and tried to envision Sophia lying over her handsome new husband's lap as he disciplined her. She was surprised at how much the thought intrigued her.

Her attention was again drawn back to the pastor's words as he described various implements that would be effective in the 'laying on of domestic discipline'. He added that it should never be done in anger and afterward, the punished wife was to be granted a clean slate, all transgressions forgiven. Faith had to admit that it made sense in that context, but she was also blushing profusely throughout the rest of the class. She peeked out of the corner of her eye, studying the pastor. He was slender but balding, which made him appear older than he was. If he approved of domestic discipline, he probably dispensed it, as well. She tried to imagine herself lying over the pastor's lap for a spanking. She shook her head, trying to erase the thought, which didn't appeal at all.

On the walk home, Faith broached the subject with Charity. "What do you think about all this domestic discipline business?"

"I had to grin, imagining big ole' Hope bending over and lifting her skirts for a paddling." Charity chuckled. "I'm not sure what I think of it in a religious context. I suppose, in some cases, it might be beneficial. What do you think? And more importantly, what do you think of Pastor Gregory as a possible husband?"

Faith refused to share her thoughts on domestic discipline, but she readily spoke up about Pastor Gregory.

"I find him to be a decent enough man. It would be interesting to be the pastor's wife and live in town, just down the street from Mrs. Barnes. I'm just not sure, though, about taking on those four motherless children."

"Children grow up, Faith. None of them are infants. Basically, you'd be feeding and clothing them. You might even enjoy it."

"I suppose," Faith replied, but she wasn't at all certain. Charity made it sound easy, but there were other factors in the raising of children—moral guidance, for one, not to mention that most siblings of her acquaintance bickered incessantly. Being exposed to such a thing on a daily basis would get on her nerves.

"Well, I think it sounds perfect for you. Promise me, you'll give it a try. At least, meet the children," Charity urged. "You know, at your age, the men who will be interested in you will either have children or grandchildren."

"That's probably true," Faith agreed. She knocked on Mrs. Reynolds' door when they got back to the boarding house.

"Yes? Oh, Faith, hello there, dear. Come on in. I'm in my housedress. I hope you don't mind."

"Not at all, Mrs. Reynolds, I'll keep this brief." Faith explained that she was willing to meet the men Mrs. Reynolds had lined up for her but would make no promises.

"That's excellent, dear. You must keep an open mind. And if you don't like the three I showed you, there are many more."

"Mrs. Reynolds, if I may ask, why have you not married one of the single men in Wyoming?"

"Actually, dear, I'm dating a man in Boston."

"Oh, I had no idea," Faith said, surprised. "He doesn't mind your spending the summers in Wyoming?"

"He understands that it's part of my life. I have no intention of changing what I do, even if we were to marry."

Later in her room, Faith had a lot to think about. Mrs. Reynolds and Hope were the two most independent women she knew, and yet they were involved with men. Charity, on the other hand, seemed to need freedom to pursue her theatrical interests. Could Faith be strong enough to build a life for herself without a man? She decided that men could come courting, but she wasn't going to rush off with the first one who came along. She would take her time and, in the meanwhile, start building her pie business. There was no reason she couldn't bake five or six pies at a time, instead of two or three. Once you had the ingredients out, it was almost the same amount of work. Then she could spend her afternoons selling them to the restaurants around town.

The satisfying notion of earning her own spending money began to flicker as a small flame within her breast, and Faith was pleased at the idea of her little nest egg growing instead of dwindling.

The next afternoon, she set off with three pies in her basket to sell, but first, she had to stop by the mercantile. She figured she'd pick the best fruit and have it set aside to pick up, once her basket was empty.

"Well, hello there. It's the pie lady," Nate said, calling to Slade.

Slade Miller came out to see Faith standing there, a bulging basket on her arm.

"Are those more pies?" he asked with a twinkle in his eye. He lifted the dishtowels covering the pies and sniffed appreciatively.

"Yes, sir, you see I've decided to sell my pies to the restaurants around town. I was wondering if I could pick out more supplies and have you hold them for me until later in the day?"

"I'll do better than that, Miss Cummings. I will take those pies off your hands, right now, and sell them here at the store."

Faith was taken aback. She had given herself a pep talk and was prepared to face her fears and visit various businesses around town. But she also felt relieved at the thought of not having to do that by selling them right here at the mercantile.

"Really? Why, I would like that." Faith, as usual, found herself completely flustered around Mr. Miller. But she remembered that she was a businesswoman now and had to negotiate prices. "H-how much would you give me for these pies?"

Mr. Miller was trying to hide a smile, as if he could see how difficult it was for Faith to speak of such matters.

"Well, let's see, I would be willing to pay a quarter per pie."

Faith eyes grew even wider. A quarter? Why, that would be well over a fifty percent profit. "You think they are worth twenty-five cents?"

"Fifty cents. Remember, I have to make a profit."

Faith nodded, realizing that whatever he paid for something, he'd turn around and sell it for twice the price. She had just had her first lesson in economics.

She stuck out her hand. "You have yourself a deal, Mr. Miller," she said, pumping his hand.

He now had a big grin on his face. "Any more pies you bake, you bring right over here to me. If these sell as well as I think they will, you might need to find yourself an industrial kitchen."

A flicker of doubt passed over Faith's face. What was an industrial kitchen? Where did one find such a place?

"It looks like you have a few questions about how things are done in the professional world, am I right?"

Faith nodded. She didn't want to show weakness in front of her new business partner, but how could she deny that the world of commerce was a mystery?

"I tell you what, why don't I take you out for dinner, tonight? We can talk about those pies of yours and figure out a plan for producing as many as possible?"

Faith nodded; that made sense. "All right, Mr. Miller. What time should I expect you?"

The store closes at five on the dot. I'll be over around 5:30 if that works for you."

"Actually," Faith replied. "If it's all right, I might as well come by and meet you here." Mr. Miller agreed that sounded like a fine idea. To her amusement, he bowed to her. Faith turned away, so that he wouldn't see her blush, and began moving around the store doing her shopping for tomorrow's pies.

It wasn't until she was on her way back to the boarding house that the full impact of her dinner plans hit her. She was having dinner with the distinguished and handsome Mr. Miller. She knew it was only a business dinner, but she could not deny that the thought made her very happy indeed.

When she got home, she found Mrs. Reynolds waiting for her with a big grin on her face. "Faith, dear, you have a caller."

Faith frowned; she was in no condition to see a visitor. She managed to remove her bonnet and pat her hair before Mrs. Reynolds was pulling her into the parlor.

"This is Mr. Olsen, you remember him?"

"Yes, of course," Faith said, nodding at Mr. Olsen as he stood. "The farmer with two grown sons."

"Dairy farmer, actually. Pleased to meet you, Miss Cummings. I would appreciate the opportunity to get to know you better."

Faith noted that Mr. Olsen had his blond hair slicked down and was holding a bouquet of rapidly-wilting wild flowers. She managed to hide a smile.

"These are for you," he said, handing her the bouquet. Faith thanked him and handed the flowers to Mrs. Reynolds, who bustled off to put them in water.

She sat down across from Mr. Olsen. He began to talk, telling her about his life. He said his son's names were Clint and Calvin. They were twins whose mother had died birthing them. His dairy farm was about an hour ride out of town. He told her about life on the dairy farm and offered to show it to her sometime.

"Thank you for asking. I shall look forward to seeing your farm," she murmured. Mr. Olsen reminded her of someone; she couldn't put her finger on who it was, though. Then she realized that it was his speech. He had the same accent as Mrs. Barnes, which made sense, because they had come from the same area. Mrs. Reynolds brought in refreshments, which Mr. Olsen consumed with relish.

"These cookies sure are good. You didn't happen to make them yourself, did you?" he asked Faith.

"Yes," she replied. "They're called Snickerdoodles. I do all the baking here at the boarding house."

"These are mighty fine," Mr. Olsen repeated. Faith would later share with Mrs. Reynolds that she was surprised by Mr. Olsen. He seemed friendlier and move lively than she had originally pegged him to be.

After about half an hour, Faith stood, and Mr. Olsen took the hint that the visit was over. "Thank you for stopping by and for the beautiful flowers, Mr. Olsen," Faith said, extending her hand.

Mr. Olsen didn't seem to know what to do with her hand. He took it in one hand and patted it with the other.

"Call me Bernard," he said and then stepped outside and tipped his hat to her, before walking down the street.

When Faith shut the door and turned around, she found both Mrs. Reynolds and Mrs. Barnes standing there smiling broadly at her.

"Well, how did it go?" Mrs. Reynolds asked.

"What did you think?" Mrs. Barnes added.

Faith laughed. "He seemed nice enough. He wants to show me his dairy farm. What more do you know about him?" she asked the two women.

"His dairy farm is quite successful, Faith. I hear he provides milk for most all of Wyoming," Mrs. Reynolds said.

"He's probably doing better than most, and you won't find anyone in town who has an unkind word to say about him, I daresay." Mrs. Barnes smiled encouragingly at Faith. "He might be the one for you. After all, has anyone else caught your eye?"

Faith did not respond. Instead, she excused herself and went to her room. Mrs. Reynolds watched her go and turned to Mrs. Barnes.

"Something is up with that young woman. I wonder if she's met someone?" she said.

Faith was not ready to share with either woman that she had feelings for Slade Miller. She had experienced enough unrequited feelings about men over the years to know it was unlikely to lead to anything, but at least he didn't frown at the sight of her anymore.

That night, as she got ready, she took extra pains with her appearance, even though it was just a business dinner. Charity came into her room to check on her and seemed surprised to see her sister sitting at the vanity and struggling to put her hair into an upswept hairdo.

"Why, Faith, do you have dinner plans?"

"Yes, I have a business dinner, if you must know," replied Faith. She didn't feel like she owed Charity any explanation of where she was going. Charity never shared her plans. But she was in too much of a hurry to play games.

"A business dinner?" Charity asked, moving behind Faith to help with her hair. "What kind of business?"

"For your information, I may be starting a pie business. I have sold some pies at the mercantile, and tonight, Mr. Miller is taking me out to discuss the future of my venture."

Charity paused for a moment and then a smile lit up her face. Quickly and deftly, she finished putting Faith's hair up, curling the dangling ends around her fingers. Faith checked her updo in her hand mirror. "It's perfect.

"You are starting a pie business? You mentioned that once in Boston, but I didn't know you were still considering it."

Faith reached into her bag and pulled out the three silver coins she had earned that day, showing them to her sister.

"How many pies did you sell to make this much money?" Charity asked, impressed.

"Three. Mr. Miller said that I should consider moving my operations to an industrial kitchen. Why, I wouldn't even know where to find such a thing."

"That might not be a bad idea, Faith. I, myself, found an old abandoned building just yesterday that was once a café. It has a kitchen, and it's just about six blocks from here. Why, you could even open up your own storefront."

Faith sat back, dazed. "How on earth would I make enough pies?"

"You would find employees and train them, of course," said

Charity as if opening a pie shop was something she was already an expert on.

"Perhaps you should come along to dinner, tonight," Faith said kindly, wondering if Charity might still be at all interested in the shopkeeper. "You and Mr. Miller could discuss it as I listen." If Charity was still interested, Faith would, of course, step aside.

Charity smiled and shook her head no. "We'll talk about it when you get home, tonight. I'll stay up. But you need to hear what Mr. Miller has to say before I add my input."

"All right," agreed Faith. "You know, Charity, if you are at all interested in Mr. Miller, this would be a good opportunity to reconnect."

"No, sister, Slade Miller is not for me. I intend to be a town character, the dramatic spinster, Miss Charity, forever wed to the theater rather than to any mere mortal man."

Faith laughed at the dramatic pose Charity had struck while uttering those words. "I doubt that, little sister. You are far too pretty to embrace a spinster lifestyle."

"He is most handsome and distinguished, though," Faith added.

This made Charity's smile widen. "Yes, he is," Charity said. "But too old for me."

"I don't think he's all that old," Faith replied.

With that, Charity bent over and whispered in her sister's ear, "Then, you marry him," a suggestion she had made before. But this time, it wasn't a sharp retort, rather a loving suggestion. Charity stood and Faith met her eyes in the mirror. For a moment, the silence hung between them until Charity went on.

"And you, too, Faith. I don't know if it's the sunlight in Wyoming or the fresh air, but you have blossomed. You've never looked prettier. I am impressed to think that you marched yourself into the mercantile and spoke to Mr. Miller about selling your pies."

"Why, thank you. It's true, I have had to overcome my shyness to get this far," Faith agreed. "I think this business venture will be good for me."

Charity escorted Faith to the door and gave her some parting advice, "Pick his brains, sister. Listen to everything he has to say. If there's anyone who knows anything about starting a business, it would be Slade."

Faith left the boarding house and started toward the mercantile. Suddenly, there was a gentleman at her side. Faith was surprised to see that it was the blacksmith, the man she had peeked in at on her first walk down Main Street.

"Why, hello," she said. "I don't believe we've met."

"Do you know who I am?" he asked, flashing his white teeth at her in a big smile.

"Yes, you're the blacksmith. I saw you in your shop one day."

"I am Yuri. Yuri Tikaani. And you are?"

"I am Faith Cummings"

"Are you new in town?"

"Yes, I came in on the bride train last week."

"But you have no husband?"

"No, my intended perished before I arrived. How long have you lived in Cheyenne?" she asked him.

"I moved here eight years ago. I was passing through, heading south, but the town was in need of a blacksmith, so I figured I'd stay for six months."

"Which became eight years?"

"That's right," Yuri agreed, smiling.

"Well, I am pleased to make your acquaintance, sir," Faith replied, stopping outside the mercantile. "And thank you for escorting me to my destination."

Mr. Tikaani looked up and saw that they were at the store. "I'm afraid the mercantile is closed, miss," he said, grinning broadly.

Before Faith could explain, Mr. Miller was at her side. Faith introduced him to the blacksmith and was surprised that the blacksmith and the merchant had little to say to one another. They exchanged hard looks until Yuri tipped his hat to Faith and walked away.

"How did you hook up with the likes of him?" Mr. Miller asked.

"He just fell in step beside me on the walk here. I don't know him at all."

"He's the blacksmith, and I suggest you stay away from that one."

"Why, what's wrong with him?"

"Just stay away from him," Slade scowled.

Faith studied his handsome countenance. It was clear that Mr. Miller did not approve of the blacksmith at all.

"Where are we going to eat?" she asked, changing the subject.

"There's a French restaurant around the corner. It's nice and quiet there. It'll be an ideal place to talk."

Faith was awestruck when they arrived at their destination. The restaurant was quite fancy, with tablecloths and candles. They didn't even order before the waiter brought the first of what they were told would be several courses.

"I don't believe I have ever dined on French food. One of the men Mrs. Reynolds is trying to match me with is opening an Italian restaurant."

Mr. Miller looked a bit taken aback, but then he started to tease. "How many men is Mrs. Reynolds trying to match you with?"

"Three, let's see, there's Pastor Gregory, Mario Martinelli, and Bernard Olsen."

"Hmm," Mr. Miller said, resting his chin on his hand. "So you could become the pastor's wife or help run your husband's Italian restaurant or become the wife of a dairy farmer."

"That's right," Faith said, impressed that Mr. Miller seemed to know most everyone in town. "And if I don't care for any of them, Mrs. Reynolds has many more in that book of hers."

"Well, the world is your oyster. So, which of those men do you prefer?"

"I've only gone to Bible study with Pastor Gregory. Mr. Olsen came calling once, and I have yet to spend any time with Mr.

Martinelli. I can tell you that I have no intention of rushing into anything or going off with the first person who asks."

"Who were you originally matched with?"

"Mr. Jaan Anderson," said Faith sorrowfully.

"Oh, yes, Jaan. He was a jovial fellow, always ready with a slap on the back and a bawdy joke. I don't know what Mrs. Reynolds was thinking. It wouldn't have been a good match. He was much too roughhewn. A refined lady like you needs a proper gentleman."

Faith was taken aback at Mr. Miller's opinion of her. She came across to him as a refined lady? Faith desperately tried to keep from blushing and quickly asked, "Which one do you think I should choose?"

"Just not the blacksmith," was Mr. Miller's surprising response. He really did not seem to like Yuri Tikaani.

As their dinner continued, they discussed the idea of Faith opening a pie business in great detail. Mr. Miller advised her not to rush into anything in that respect, either. Selling her pies at the mercantile for a while would be a good indication of the demand for them. Faith was relieved; she wasn't really ready to start producing on a major scale yet. She wanted to spend at least an entire year in Wyoming to observe how the seasons played out before she took the plunge of opening a business.

"What is it like in the Wyoming territory in the winter?" she asked.

"Snow and ice, folks get snowed in. My business drops off a bit from December through March, although when people do make it into town, they stock up heavily. It can be unpredictable, especially for those folks up in the higher elevations. I've seen snow storms as early as October and as late as April."

Faith realized that if business in town dropped off, the demand for her pies would, as well, and said as much to Mr. Miller.

"Possibly. We'll just have to wait and see. We'll go over your sales and compare notes at the end of your first year."

"You'll keep track of how many pies I sell?" she asked, surprised.

"I keep track of everything I sell. I need to know how many vegetables to put in on the farm."

"You have a farm?" Faith asked, again surprised. "I just assumed you lived atop the mercantile."

"I do live on the third floor, but that may change some day. The farm is close to town, and I have a family running it for me. I grow a lot of the produce I sell at the store. Other local farmers bring in their produce and eggs to round it out."

At hearing this surprising news, Faith began to look at Mr. Miller, the gentleman farmer, a bit differently.

"And do you have livestock on the ranch?" she asked, her eyes wide.

"I have forty-five head of sheep," Mr. Miller said, enjoying her surprised expression. "Why does that surprise you? Just last week, I didn't come in to the store for a couple days because it was shearing time."

The thought occurred to Faith that perhaps Charity might have found Mr. Miller more attractive if she'd known he was an actual cowboy and gentleman farmer. After dinner, he escorted her to the boarding house.

They agreed on the stroll home that for the time being, she would continue to make pies in the kitchen at the boarding house and bring them to the mercantile. They would keep an eye on the rise and fall of sales during the four seasons and come up with a five-year plan for expansion.

All too soon, they had arrived at the boarding house. Faith and Slade climbed the steps to the door, then Faith turned to look up at her escort. He was so handsome in the moonlight that her heart caught in her throat.

He leaned close and tilted Faith's chin up. "Do you think you could learn to call me Slade?" he asked gently.

"Why, Mr. Mil...Slade," she said, catching herself mid-word. "I, well, I'm not certain that would be proper."

"Why ever not? We are, after all, business partners, as well as friends." Then Slade did the most curious thing. He leaned in and kissed her, right on the lips. It wasn't just a quick peck, either. It was a full, passionate kiss. Not that Faith had anything to compare it with; she had never been kissed before, not like that. Faith's eyes closed and remained that way. Even when he had pulled away, the feel of his lips pressed against hers still lingered on. Suddenly, her eyes snapped open. Tongue-tied, Faith backed away.

"I'll be looking forward to seeing you at the mercantile tomorrow," Slade said, turning to walk away. He turned back to wave for a moment.

Faith tentatively waved her hand, overcome at the sensation of receiving her very first kiss. She went inside and found Charity in her room.

"How did the date go?" Charity asked, inviting her in.

"Business dinner," Faith corrected her. "We went to the French restaurant around the corner from the mercantile."

"Sounds pretty fancy for a business dinner."

"Charity!" Faith replied, shocked. "It was just business, I swear. After considering expansion, Slade and I agreed that I should wait at least a year before enlarging my operations. In the meantime, I will continue to produce pies and sell them at the mercantile."

"That sounds like a sensible plan," Charity agreed. "And now, Mr. Miller has become Slade?" she asked, hiding a smile.

"Well, we are business partners," Faith replied, flustered. She fled before her sister could inquire further about the evening. She needed time to think about all that had transpired. Slade Miller was turning out to be quite a surprise. They were attracted to one another, that much was undeniable. If he was interested, none of those other men Mrs. Reynolds had shown her would hold a candle to Slade. But Faith was not secure enough to announce to the matchmaker or her sister or to anyone else in Cheyenne that she had a beau. A goodnight kiss did not amount to a proposal of marriage.

No, she scolded herself, the sensible thing to do was to continue to meet the men who came calling and then, when someone proposed, she would take it from there. Besides, she reasoned, if Slade was indeed interested, he would be more likely to come forward if she were being courted by others than if she sat at home dreaming about him.

She got ready for bed and lay in the dark imagining the different paths laid out before her. Turn one way, and she was the wife of a dairy farmer, living near her sister, Hope. Turn another, and she was the pastor's wife, listening to him rehearse his sermons, mothering his children. Perhaps what awaited her was a life at her husband's side running a restaurant and being part of a large, Italian family, or she might become the wife of the mercantile owner, helping him with his farm and store and selling her pies. It took Faith a long time to fall asleep that night.

CHAPTER 8

ednesday night, Faith was walking home after Bible study. Pastor Gregory had asked to escort her, but there were too many people lingering at the church, and she didn't want to set tongues to wagging. Charity had not joined her for this particular class. In fact, she hadn't seen her since early that morning. Faith fretted about her little sister. Where was she? How would she know if Charity went missing? And when would she report it? She made a mental note to insist that her sister at least tell her who her local acquaintances were. She didn't understand why Charity had to be so secretive. As she turned the corner and walked past some bushes, she felt a hand grab her arm and pull her into the shadows. She shrieked in terror.

"Shhh," Yuri, the blacksmith said, covering her mouth with his hand. With a wide smile, he held a finger to his lips. She smiled back at him, and he removed his hand.

"Where are you coming from, Faith Cummings?" he asked, accompanied by a doff of his hat.

"Bible study. You should try it. It was very interesting this week."

"I'll save that treat for later in life. I'm afraid I'd fall asleep if I tried to take a class after a hard day's work."

"Of course, of course," Faith said. "I'm sorry I screamed, but you startled me."

"And I'm sorry I didn't alert you that I was lurking behind that bush before I pounced," Yuri apologized.

Faith laughed and took Mr. Tikaani's arm when he offered it. They ran across the street, out of sight of the church.

"A warm summer night, if only we could have ice cream," he said, looking up at the full moon.

"Ice cream? Where on earth would we get that?" Faith asked, puzzled.

"I think I know," he said. "Follow me."

With that, he turned to the left and led her down an alley to a store that was lit up. Inside, they were selling dishes of ice cream. '

"What a treat," Faith said.

Mr. Tikaani got them both a bowl, and they sat outside on little iron chairs to eat.

"I've had ice cream before, of course," she said. "But usually only once a year, at the fourth of July church social."

"They do the same thing here," said Yuri. "But in the meantime, you can get it any time at this shop in the evenings."

"Good to know," said Faith. "Although I think that having ice cream whenever one wanted to would make it less exciting than to have it just once a year."

Yuri laughed; he seemed to find just about everything Faith said to be highly amusing. Faith came to the realization that perhaps an attraction to someone had more to do with how they saw you than how you saw them. If Mr. Tikaani found her to be amusing company, she would, of course, seek him out.

As they ate their ice cream, they told each other about their lives. Faith spoke of Boston and her family, Yuri, of learning to be a blacksmith from his father in northern Canada. When they finished, he rose to escort her home. Faith could not help admiring him. Besides being a very handsome man, his physique was strong, his arms bulging with muscles. Although he had a shirt on, this particular evening, Faith had never before seen him wearing much more than undershirt and trousers, a vest and apron.

He led her towards the boarding house, and at the door, he proved to be a perfect gentleman. There was no attempt at a kiss. Faith felt very safe with Mr. Tikaani, despite Slade's warnings. She opened the door to the boarding house and turned to say good night.

"I believe that you and I should go to dinner one evening soon, Miss Cummings," Mr. Tikaani said. His voice was deep. His accent brought to mind glaciers and northern wilderness.

"Perhaps another time," Faith said, bidding him a good night.

Yuri doffed his hat to her and walked away, smiling.

Mrs. Reynolds had been coming down the stairs just in time to see Yuri's departure. For the second time that evening, Faith found herself grabbed by the upper arm and pulled somewhere. Mrs. Reynolds shut the parlor door behind them and began to speak. Actually, it would be more accurate to say that she began to scold.

"Faith, do you remember my telling you that you need to tell me about any men who approach you?"

"Yes, Mrs. Reynolds. Is this about Mr. Tikaani? He's very nice, but I'm not interested in him romantically."

"Yes, he's quite good looking, but the word around town is that he has a wife and family in northern Canada. He is looking for an American wife to secure his citizenship. Would that be a situation you'd wish to be involved in?"

"No, of course not," Faith replied, taken aback. "I had no idea."

"Did you, in any way, encourage him?" Mrs. Reynolds asked, peering intently into Faith's eyes. "This is not a man to toy with, Faith. Be very careful. The slightest encouragement could have disastrous repercussions."

Faith opened her mouth, prepared to testify to Mr. Tikaani's good character but then realized that Mrs. Reynolds was not expecting a response. She began to feel guilty; she had not mentioned Mr. Miller to Mrs. Reynolds, either.

Mrs. Reynolds caught the look of uncertainty flicker across Faith's face. She showed Faith to a chair and sat across to her.

"Faith, I have begun to suspect that there is someone on the scene that has caught your eye. If so, now is the time to tell me."

Faith ducked her head, embarrassed. She was reluctant to talk about her attraction to Mr. Miller out loud with anyone until she was sure of his interest, but she longed to discuss it with someone and found herself saying the words she had held in her heart out loud. "I-I have a secret, Mrs. Reynolds. I'm embarrassed to share it with you."

Mrs. Reynolds leaned forward and placed her hand over Faith's. "Whatever it is, dear, you can trust me. Not a word about your confession will ever pass my lips."

"I am very attracted to a certain gentleman. Much more so than any of the other gentlemen who are interested in courting me. But I'm not sure if my interest is returned, although he did kiss me one time."

"This gentleman kissed you? Are we speaking of someone here in Cheyenne?" Mrs. Reynolds asked.

Faith nodded. "It's Mr. Slade Miller," she whispered, in case anyone walking past the door could overhear.

Mrs. Reynolds leaned back, surprised. "Mr. Miller? When did this all come about? Tell me all about it!"

"Well, there isn't much to tell. I went by the mercantile and apologized for Charity. I wanted him to know about her broken engagement and that she wasn't ready for another relationship. He was cold and indifferent when he discovered I was her sister, so I decided to bake him one of my pies."

"And did that help soften Mr. Miller's attitude?" Mrs. Reynolds asked.

"Well, I guess he liked it, because he decided that perhaps the Cummings girls were not so bad, after all. As you know, I've been selling my pies at the mercantile, so it's only natural that I'm there every day. Sometimes, I even help out behind the counter. One night, he asked me out for dinner, strictly to discuss my pie baking business."

"Of course," Mrs. Reynolds agreed, a smile flickering about the corners of her mouth.

"He took me to that French restaurant around the corner from the mercantile. Afterward, after he walked me home, he took me in his arms and h-he..." Faith began to flush at the memory of Mr. Miller's lips pressed against hers.

"He what, dear?" Mrs. Reynolds asked.

"He kissed me," Faith whispered once again.

"My, my," said Mrs. Reynolds. "I wondered why you weren't more interested in the men I was showing you. It's Mr. Slade Miller you've given your heart to. I do believe I matched him with the wrong sister."

Faith began to protest. "Oh, I'm not the type to give my heart away because of a kiss," she began to protest, but then she realized that Mrs. Reynolds didn't appear to believe her. Her voice trailed off and she gave a slight nod. While she felt uncomfortable sharing her most intimate thoughts with someone else, it was a relief to finally speak the words out loud.

"Please don't tell him that I spoke to you, promise me," Faith said. "He hasn't asked to come courting. I don't know what to think; does he really like me, or was he just being polite? What do you think?"

"I promise to never tell anyone what you've told me, especially Slade Miller. But I can't guarantee that if our paths cross, I won't discuss you with him. Only if he brings you up, of course."

Faith looked uncertain and worried.

"It's all right, dear. I have managed to coax along many a courtship without estranging the participants. Sometimes men need to be reminded of the rules of courtship in polite society, that's all."

Faith began to feel better. It helped to have someone to talk to about her concerns. And Mrs. Reynolds certainly had a lot of experience in affairs of the heart.

"Hmm," said Mrs. Reynolds, tapping her chin with one long-nailed finger. "I guess we'll just have to wait and see if Mr. Miller should make his intentions known," she advised.

She assured the matchmaker once again that she would not encourage the blacksmith and headed up to her room. As she passed Charity's room, she could see a light under the door.

She knocked and whispered, "Open up, Charity, it's me."

Her sister opened the door, looking tired and distracted. Over Charity's shoulder, Faith could see piles of papers on her desk and on her bed.

"Charity, what's going on?" Faith asked.

"If you want to talk, let's go to your room. Mine's a mess," Charity said, shutting the door behind her.

They moved to her room. "Immaculate as always," Charity said, looking around with appreciation.

"I'd be glad to help you tidy your room, Charity," Faith offered.

"Leave my stuff alone," Charity said, and they both burst into laughter. This was a conversation they'd had many, many times over the years.

"What were all those papers, Charity?" Faith asked.

"Schematics for the opera house, Faith. What else would they be?" Charity snapped.

"I'm not prying, little sister. I'm just wondering how you are doing. I see you so seldom," Faith replied, hurt by Charity's tone of voice.

Charity ran her fingers through her hair. "Of course, I'm sorry, it's just that I'm exhausted from working so hard on this project."

"Is there a hurry?"

"A hurry? What do you mean?" Charity replied.

"A hurry to get the opera house open? You have to expect that it's going to take a few years."

"Years!" Charity said. "Years? I can't wait years to perform again."

"Well, you don't need to have a theater to perform, do you? Do you remember after the bridal train weddings, someone performed a Shakespeare soliloquy?"

Charity sat back down. "I hadn't thought of that."

"Also, did you know that there is a stage in the back of the church?"

"There is?"

"Yes, check it out when we are at Bible study. It's that curtained area behind the altar. It is set up for nativity performances and such. It could serve as a performance venue."

Charity stared at Faith as if she were seeing her for the first time. "That's brilliant, Faith. I'll look into it. It could serve as a stop gap until the funds for the opera house are in place."

"And how are you raising these funds?" Faith asked.

"What are you insinuating?" Charity asked, now defensive.

Faith sighed; keeping up with Charity's mood swings could be exhausting.

"Charity, I am your older sister. I like to think I played no small part in raising you. I am very concerned when you disappear for hours at a time. Please tell me who you are associating with here in Cheyenne. What if you should go missing?"

Chastened, Charity came over and sat beside her sister. She put her arms around Faith and rested her head against hers.

"You did raise me, Faith, I barely remember Mother. I know I'm not the proper young lady you wished I would be. For your information, I have been going out with some of the men whom Mrs. Reynolds is fixing me up with. Also, I have been attending upper crust events, galas, and fund raisers, in order to meet the wealthy people in Cheyenne.

"Why have you never told me of this? I would have been willing to go with you. Even though you are of age, Charity, you should be chaperoned."

"Oh, Faith, this is 1890, not the dark ages. It would be a disaster to bring you along. You'd be shy and uncomfortable, hiding in a corner somewhere. You aren't the mingling type."

"I can't deny that, and I'm glad you are meeting the men Mrs. Reynolds has for you. Who have you met?"

"Never mind about that, no one of interest. What about you and Pastor Gregory? What's going on with that?"

"I met his children at church. They seem well behaved, three girls and a quiet little boy."

"Sounds perfect," Charity enthused.

"I'm not certain. The pastor seems like a good man, but he believes in domestic discipline, remember?"

"Faith," a bemused Charity replied, "I believe that most of the men out west believe in domestic discipline. If you tried it, you might even like it."

"Charity!" Faith said, shocked to the core. "Like being spanked? I can't even imagine such a thing."

"You have to let men be men," was Charity's cryptic response. "And who else have you met?"

"Bernard Olsen, the dairy farmer. He's not as serious as he first appears, once you get to know him. He came here one day and brought flowers. I'm going to dinner at his dairy farm one of these days. I understand that it's near Hope and Noble's ranch."

"And what about the third man; wasn't there a third?"

Faith thought for a moment. "Ah, yes, Mr. Martinelli. He must be very busy getting his restaurant open. He hasn't come calling yet."

"Have you thought about dropping by to see the place? I'm sure he would love to give you a tour."

"I would never do any such thing without being invited."

"This isn't Boston, Faith. Loosen up," Charity replied. "Well, so far, it sounds like the pastor is the front runner. Have you met anyone besides those three?"

"Yes, Mr. Tikaani, the blacksmith."

Charity looked puzzled. "I've seen him before, and he doesn't appear to be your type."

"I didn't realize I had a type," Faith replied.

"You know what I mean. I don't believe he'd be right for you,"

"Mrs. Reynolds said that there is a rumor he has a family in Canada."

"Well, then, he's definitely not for you. Be careful, sister," Charity said. She released Faith and kissed her on the cheek and then stood.

"I've got to go back to work. But thanks for the tip about the stage in the back of the church. That was very helpful."

And with that, Charity was gone. When Faith went over their conversation later, she realized that she had done most of the talking. She hadn't learned anything about Charity's activities at all.

CHAPTER 9

*F*aith was standing behind the counter of the mercantile, smiling at the customers and answering any questions they might ask. She was surprised at how much she enjoyed helping out at the shop. Interacting with folks in a professional capacity proved to be much easier than in social settings.

She was arranging some canisters on the counter when the door bells jangled. She looked up to see Doreen and Dobie walking towards her, Doreen smiling widely.

"Hello, Doreen, how are you two?" Faith asked, glad to see one of her fellow brides.

"How are you, Miss Faith?" Doreen asked. She grabbed Dobie by the hand and pulled him over to stand in front of Faith. "Dobie, here, has been made foreman of the ranch! We have our own cabin and are here for supplies. Mr. Gunderson let us use the horse and buggy for the day."

"Well, congratulations, Dobie," Faith said as Dobie blushed pink with a mixture of pride and embarrassment. Faith took one of her pies off the counter and said, "My gift to the two of you for a celebration dinner, tonight."

"Did you bake this yourself?" Dobie asked, impressed.

Faith nodded.

"You'll have to show me how to make one of those," Doreen added. She put her hand protectively over her stomach.

"Are you? You're not?" Faith began to ask, doing calculations in her head. Was it possible that Doreen was already pregnant?

"I think I just might be expecting. We're going to see Doc Neesan while I'm here, to find out for sure."

"Well, my goodness," Faith said. "You don't waste any time, young lady."

Doreen laughed as Dobie wandered off to look at farm supplies.

"How about you, Faith? Have you found anyone yet?" Doreen asked.

Just then, Slade walked out from the back and began to move behind Faith, arranging items on the counter.

"Mr. Miller, please come meet one of the young ladies I traveled here from Boston with."

Slade spun around on his heel and put out his hand. "You were on the bride train?" he asked.

Doreen's eyes grew wide as she looked at Faith and Mr. Miller standing side-by-side behind the counter.

"Yes, Mr. Miller. I was the youngest bride on the train. And this is my new husband, Dobie."

Dobie walked over and shook hands with Mr. Miller. He asked a question about a farming implement, and the two men wandered over to the that section of the store to compare items.

Doreen leaned in and whispered, "I wondered why you were working behind the counter. Are you interested in your sister's ex-fiancé?"

Faith looked around, relieved that they seemed to have the front room of the store to themselves, so no one could have overheard. "I...what? Why ever do you think that?" she asked, flustered.

"Don't worry, it's not obvious, just something I wondered about. You two make a nice-looking couple there behind the counter. Come here," Doreen said, leaning over the counter as if to whisper something to Faith. Faith leaned towards her, and all of a sudden, Doreen reached out and pulled Faith's hair out of its bun. Faith, startled, straightened and tried to grab the ribbon that had held her hair up back from Doreen.

"Why did you…" she began to ask when the two men returned, Dobie holding a branding iron.

Faith stood up stock still, blushing because her hair was down around her shoulders instead of up in its usual tidy bun.

"You've got to advertise the merchandise," Doreen whispered, winking at Faith.

Mr. Miller came behind the counter to once again stand next to Faith.

"Your new assistant is very pretty," Doreen said as innocently as possible.

"My what?" Slade asked and then realized she was referring to Faith. He turned and really looked at Faith, seemingly for the first time. He took in the long, soft hair, pink cheeks, shy demeanor and, suddenly, couldn't take his eyes off of her. Unnerved, he turned and walked to the back of the store.

"I can't believe you did that," Faith seethed, once more trying to grab her hair ribbon from Doreen.

"You have to let a man see you at your most fetching," said Doreen. "You can thank me later." She giggled as she began to order the amounts of flour, sugar, and eggs she needed.

As she and Dobie paid for their purchases, she slipped the hair ribbon back to Faith and waved a sassy goodbye over her shoulder as they left the store.

Deeply embarrassed, Faith reached back to put her hair back into its bun. Mr. Miller came back out from behind the shop and took his place again behind the counter.

"What are you doing?" he asked Faith, staring at her curiously.

"Trying to put my hair up; it came down and, well—"

"Leave it. I like it," said Slade.

"Well, I must be going," Faith said as casually as she could muster, eager to flee.

"Yes, of course, have a good day," he called out to her as she rushed out of the shop, putting her bonnet on.

"My new assistant." Slade chuckled to himself. Then he grew serious as he considered the notion.

Faith rushed home to finish her baking and to pull herself together. She was going to the pastor's house for dinner and to meet his children. At the appointed time, she put one of her pies in her basket and walked to the church. The pastor and his family inhabited the house behind the church.

She knocked on the door and could hear some shushing on the other side. Finally, the door opened, and the oldest daughter stood there. Faith recognized the look in her eye. This young girl had taken on responsibility for her younger siblings, as she herself had done when her mother died. The daughter, being very proper, stepped back and let Faith enter.

"Just a moment," she said. "I'll get Pa." She went to find her father, and soon there were three additional children staring up at Faith. She could hear pots and pans clanking in the kitchen, but the pastor came from the opposite direction.

He extended his hand and greeted Faith warmly.

"Line up, children. Here is Eve, and this is Ruth," he said, introducing the children. "This is my youngest daughter, Sarah, and here," he said, pulling a little boy over to stand beside his sisters, "is Daniel."

"Well, hello," Faith said, leaning over to shake hands with each of the children. Politely, they put out their hands and gave her a shake in return.

"Aunt Edna," Godwin called. "Come here and meet our dinner guest."

The pastor's elderly aunt came from the back, wiping her hands on her apron.

"How do you do, dear?" she asked, giving Faith a grimace of a smile. The aunt appeared to be in pain, pressing her free hand against her lower back. "Have a seat; dinner will be ready shortly."

"I brought a pie," Faith offered, holding out her basket.

Edna took the pie and looked relieved.

"You can have it later, if you've already planned dessert," Faith offered.

"We'll have it tonight; my bread pudding didn't quite set up," Edna replied. She headed back to the kitchen.

"Can I help?" Faith called after her.

"No, no, have a seat," the pastor said, showing Faith to a floral chintz chair. "You are, after all, the guest of honor."

"Guest of honor," little Daniel repeated, hopping up and down.

"Let me tell you about the children. Eve, here, is almost finished with school. She's gone much further than the rest of the children her age," he said. "And she plays the harp like an angel."

Eve added that she was twelve years of age. She had long brown curls and blue eyes.

"Ruth and Sarah are both good little musicians, too. Ruth plays the piano, and Sarah is learning the violin."

Faith smiled at the middle sisters. They each stepped forward as their big sister had done and announced their ages, ten and eight. Both girls had pale, straight blonde hair and matching dresses with bows on them.

"And Daniel is five, and—" he began.

Daniel piped up, interrupting his father, "I'm an artist." He was as proud as punch with his announcement.

"Yes, well,..." the pastor began again, but Daniel grabbed Faith by the hand and took her over to a large book, which turned out to be the family Bible. He began to open the pages and took out a picture he had drawn.

"Here's Noah and his family and his ark, and this is a boy bear with a girl bear."

Faith was honestly impressed; she had expected to see basic

stick figures, but instead, his characters had facial features and hair and clothing. Noah's Ark had an arch over it.

"That's the rainbow, see, and here is the dove bringing the olive branch," he said, pointing to a little V in the sky.

"That is very good, Daniel," Faith enthused, honestly impressed.

Just then, Aunt Edna announced that dinner was ready.

The family gathered around the table. Pastor Gregory led them in grace as everyone held hands around the table. Faith could feel that the pastor's hand was perspiring; he was clearly nervous.

They ate the stuffed, baked chicken with corn and zucchini. Daniel asked where the potatoes were, and Edna confessed that she'd forgotten to cook them.

Daniel sighed. Edna looked weary, and the girls didn't seem surprised. The dinner conversation was sparse.

Finally, one of the littler girls asked, "What kind of pie did you bring?"

"Apple pie," said Faith, and the children looked pleased.

Faith studied the children as they ate. Little Daniel was a tiny duplicate of his father, and Eve had his features, as well. *The two blondes must resemble their mother*, Faith thought.

"Our mother—" Sarah began, but she was hushed by a look from her two older sisters.

"Oh, I'd like to hear all about your mother," Faith said kindly. "Do you look like her?"

This seemed to bring the children to life, and they began to talk about their beloved mother. It turned out that Ruth and Sarah did, indeed, resemble their mother, who had died two years prior. Daniel shared sadly that he could hardly remember her.

"Was your mother musical?" Faith asked. She knew the pastor could sing, had heard his voice rise above the others when singing in church.

"Mummy played the piano," said Sarah. "Pa plays the violin."

"Like you do," Faith added, which seemed to please Sarah.

After dinner, the pastor sent his aunt to bed, saying he would clean up.

Edna looked relieved as she headed toward the back of the house. They went and sat in the front room, and the children performed for Faith. She marveled at how accomplished they were, including little Daniel, who sang along as his sisters played. Afterward, they said goodnight and went upstairs without being asked by their father. Daniel seemed to want to stay, but Eve picked him up and carried him upstairs.

"Let's go tackle those dishes, shall we?" Faith asked.

"Oh, no, I'll do them after you leave," said the pastor.

"Nonsense," said Faith. "I couldn't concentrate, knowing the dishes were sitting there getting cold and sticky."

Soon, they were standing, elbow to elbow, Faith washing and the pastor drying. Faith was surprised at how comfortable she felt.

"Did you enjoy meeting the children?" the pastor asked.

"Yes, thank you, Pastor Gregory."

"Call me Godwin," he replied.

"I did very much, Godwin. The girls are so well mannered, and little Daniel seems very sweet."

"I was very like him as a child. I hope he'll follow in my footsteps, but little people do seem to have a mind of their own."

Faith laughed. "Well, he is a good artist for his age. I mean, some people never outgrow the stick figure phase, and he has already gone way beyond that."

"Do you think so? Hmm, perhaps I should encourage his art more."

"I do; there were several museums in Boston, and I used to visit them regularly."

By then, the dishes were done and put away. Godwin showed Faith into the parlor.

"Would you like a cup of tea?" he asked.

"I think not. I really enjoyed seeing your house and meeting the children, Godwin," Faith said. "They seem very well behaved."

Godwin seemed pleased by this. "I'm doing the best I can, and I don't know what we'd do without Aunt Edna, but the girls could use the influence of a well-mannered lady, such as yourself."

"Of course, of course," said Faith. "Well, I really must go."

The pastor retrieved her shawl and walked her to the boarding house.

"Are the children all right by themselves?"

"Eve is very responsible, and Edna is there, if need be," he explained.

When she got to the porch, she turned. "Thank you for a lovely evening. Your children are charming. I very much enjoyed getting to know them better," she repeated. Faith was surprised to realize that she meant it.

The pastor chuckled. "I don't know how charming they are, but they did behave well, tonight." Then he got serious. "I'm glad you stayed on in Wyoming, you know." He took her hand, lifted it to his lips, and kissed it.

Faith smiled, deeply touched. She could tell he was a good man, earnest, humble and sincere. She had prayed over the years for God to send her a man such as this.

"Shall we go to dinner alone, next time?" he asked.

"That would be very nice," Faith agreed with a nod.

Godwin looked relieved at that.

After he took his leave and she shut the door behind her, Faith was surprised that Mrs. Barnes and Mrs. Reynolds weren't waiting to descend upon her. She wandered into the kitchen, but the lights were off, the house quiet.

Faith smiled to herself. The fact that the ladies were giving her some space meant they knew this could be serious and didn't want to intrude. If it weren't for Slade Miller...but Faith made herself stop her thoughts from traveling down that path. The shop owner was a wild card, possibly an unrequited crush. The pastor was real —someone who was forthcoming about his interest and his intentions. Faith had known, meeting his children, that she could handle being their mother. The girls needed a woman younger than their Aunt Edna, to guide them as they entered young womanhood. And little Daniel, the delicate, sensitive little fellow, needed an advocate as he pursued his creativity, in spite of his pragmatic father's wishes. Yes, this was a family who needed her, a life she knew she could step into. And perhaps the pastor would help guide her willful sister Charity, just eighteen and not quite a woman yet. Perhaps Charity would live with them. Godwin had shared that his Aunt Edna had raised her own children, and now, her deceased niece's children. She needed to spend the rest of her days not being responsible for anyone but herself.

As Faith climbed the steps to her room, she saw a light under Charity's door. That meant that her sister was safely home and getting ready for bed. She tapped lightly on the door.

"Oh, hello, sister," Charity said, hugging her. "Come in."

"You cleaned your room!" Faith said, surprised.

Charity laughed. "Yes, I did. Guess what?"

"I have no idea," Faith said, but whatever Charity's news was, it seemed to have had a calming effect upon her high-strung sister.

"I have officially been made a member of the committee forming to open the opera house. And guess what else?"

"What?" she asked, relieved that Charity was no longer trying to build a theater, herself.

"It's a paying position, Faith. I'm going to be the head of the fundraising department."

"You don't say," said Faith. "That's wonderful, Charity. I mean it. This way, you'll be able to make sure the new building suits your needs."

"Exactly! I'm glad you can see how important this is," Charity said and then seemed to remember something. "Your dinner with the pastor, how did it go?"

"He's a nice man, and his children are very sweet. Three girls, ranging in age from eight to twelve. Then there's little Daniel, the youngest. He's a sweet boy who wants to be an artist."

"Sounds perfect!" Charity enthused. "I'm so glad it went well. I've seen the aunt who helps him with the children and she seems a bit elderly for the task. I'm sure a wife is badly needed. In fact, I'm surprised Mrs. Reynolds didn't match you with him, in the first place."

Faith kissed her sister goodnight and headed back to her room. She knew why the matchmaker hadn't placed her with the minister. Four children, and Faith had not particularly wanted any. But if things didn't work out with Slade, and there was a very real possibility they wouldn't, the pastor was indeed, as Charity had once said, the front runner for her hand.

CHAPTER 10

Sunday at church, Pastor Gregory spoke of an end-of-summer county fair at the fairgrounds on the outskirts of Cheyenne. He asked for volunteers to man the bake sale the church always held as a fundraiser. He also said that the fair would culminate with a dance on the last night.

After services, the young women in the parish were atwitter with excitement. They sounded like a flock of birds as they chirped about which dress they would wear to the dance and how they would fix their hair. Faith waited in line to talk to Pastor Gregory. Charity had called him the frontrunner for Faith's affections, and besides, Slade had not approached her further. Oh, she saw him on her daily trips to the mercantile and he always had a special smile for her, but he had not come calling. There had been no further invitations to dinner. She had decided that he must not be interested in her.

After speaking with Charity, the night she went to dinner, Faith had begun to daydream about becoming the pastor's wife, getting the children off to school in the mornings, listening to him practice his sermons, living just down the street from Mrs. Barnes. When it was her turn to speak to the pastor, she fixed him with her biggest smile. She watched a flush creep up the pastor's neck until it covered his face as he smiled back at her. She had her answer—he really did seem to care for her. It wouldn't be just a marriage of convenience.

"Will you be attending the dance, Miss Cummings?" he asked formally, in case anyone overheard.

"I believe I will, Pastor Gregory," she replied. "I'd like to volunteer to help with the bake sale."

"See Mrs. Michaels; she is chairing the committee. It's a huge fundraiser for the church, and with a donation of some of your pies, we could break records."

She agreed and gave him another smile as she turned to walk away.

"How are things going between you and the pastor?" Hope asked, walking up beside her.

"Shhh," Faith said, looking about to see if anyone had overheard.

"What's the big deal?" Hope asked. "It's not like it's a sin for two people to keep company."

"I would prefer to keep public speculation about my love life to a minimum. Where is Mr. Noble?" Faith asked, changing the subject.

"He went to get the carriage. We really enjoy it when you and Charity come for Sunday supper."

"Do you think he really likes us?" Faith asked.

"I do. He asks about you and seems to enjoy hearing stories about the three of us growing up together. Say, have you seen any of the other brides around town?" Hope asked. "I'm so isolated on the ranch, I don't get to hear about people."

"I see little Doreen once in a while. I believe she's expecting, already. I thought I saw the Spanish twins riding on the back of a wagon, but they were way down the street, so I couldn't be sure. And Edith and Helga are standing over there with their husbands."

"No word of the others?"

"Mrs. Reynolds says that everything seems to be working out.

She says these mail order marriages, by and large, turn out quite well. Isn't that amazing?"

"A miracle," agreed Hope. "Who is that Charity is talking to?" she asked, nodding in their sister's direction.

Faith looked closely. She was talking to a young cowboy. He almost resembled her long-lost fiancé, Thomas. Faith and Hope looked at each other and then looked back again, but he'd disappeared into the crowd.

"It couldn't have been Thomas, could it?" asked Faith.

"I have no idea, but I intend to find out," said Hope.

That night at dinner, the girls questioned their little sister carefully.

"What young man? I'm sure any resemblance was all in your imagination," she assured them.

Faith decided to believe her, but she knew Hope wouldn't let the matter rest.

All too soon, the county fair was upon them. Faith had Charity help her produce a couple dozen pies for the bake sale and several dozen little "hand pies" that people could eat right then and there. Mrs. Reynolds and Mrs. Barnes did some baking, as well, turning out cookies and brownies. On the day of the fair, the women took Mrs. Barnes' buggy, loaded with goodies, to the fairgrounds to set up.

"Are you going to tonight's dance?" Faith asked Charity.

"Perhaps, I haven't decided," she replied with a toss of her curls.

"I have never seen a young woman so disinterested in romance," Mrs. Barnes clucked.

"It's not that I'm disinterested, just not quite ready," Charity replied.

They arrived at the make-shift fairgrounds and quickly found their booth. By pulling together with the other ladies in their parish, they were ready for business in no time. As the day wore on, Faith's pies sold out in record time. Her small "hand pies" had also been a big seller.

Mr. Martinelli had single handedly eaten three of them and had proposed on the spot, declaring that the two of them would make a dynamic team running the Italian restaurant. She had giggled, knowing it was all in jest, or at least hoping he was jesting. Afterward, Faith could not stop smiling at the thought she had so many interested suitors that she could take a proposal of marriage, even one made in jest, lightly.

By the end of the day, Mrs. Michaels was certain they'd made more money for the church than ever before. Faith had very much enjoyed manning the booth and chatting with the people. It reminded her of helping out at the mercantile. She discovered that working gave her a professional reason to interact with people and took away some of her shyness.

Charity and Mrs. Barnes urged Faith to go to the dance once they had shut down for the day. She felt bad leaving the rest of the ladies to break down the booth but could not deny that she wanted to at least see the dance. She'd been told that there would be someone 'calling' the steps and they would be 'high-stepping' and 'do-si-doing'. She just had to see what a do-si-do was.

The dance floor was a stage set on a wooden riser. There were lanterns hanging from the tree branches overhead, and it was all very festive. Faith was fascinated by the band. She was accustomed to the string quartets she had heard in Boston. This band was very home spun, playing an assortment of instruments she wasn't familiar with. There was something that looked like a violin, but they called it a fiddle, someone was playing what appeared to be a washboard, another was blowing into a small wooden mouthpiece, and another person was drumming on an overturned metal bucket. The music was loud and lively, though, and soon, she was clapping along and stomping her feet like everyone else.

Everyone seemed to be dancing in fours. There was a lot of arm linking and spinning, but she couldn't grasp the steps. Hands pulled her out onto the dance floor and she tried to follow along, finally picking up some of the patterns. At one point, she was caught up into a strong set of male arms.

"Mr. Tikaani!" she said, shocked to find that it was the blacksmith and he wasn't doing the steps everyone else was doing. He was pressed up against her and moving slowly. There was a look in his eye that she found alarming and she could smell alcohol on his breath.

"Stop, stop please," she insisted, pushing him away. His chest was massive, an unmovable force.

"What is the problem, Faith Cummings?" he said, pulling her up against him and breathing into her hair.

"Mr. Tikaani…" Faith had given the blacksmith a wide berth whenever she'd seen him since she discovered he already had a family in Canada.

"Yuri," he corrected her.

"I don't want to dance with you," she said, too flustered to couch the words in a more sensitive way. This took him by surprise and, with a final shove, she was able to push him away and run down the steps, heading back towards the safety of the booth area. But Mr. Tikaani followed, Faith could hear the heavy fall of his footsteps behind her. When she sped up, so did he, and as soon as they passed some low-hanging branches, he pushed her into the brush. He pulled her against him, planting his lips on hers. Faith turned her head away and pushed against the blacksmith, but his grip was strong, his body a hard wall of muscle.

"Stop, please stop. Get away. No, no, no," she cried out, her voice level rising in intensity.

"You will not refuse me, Faith Cummings," he said, his voice low and threatening. Faith screamed as he pushed her to the ground and lay atop her. She pushed at him, clawing his face, frantically screaming for help. Suddenly, she felt the weight of the blacksmith lifted off her. She watched as a tall dark figure, his shadow between her and the moon, punched the blacksmith. As they tussled, she realized it was Slade. He was taller than the blacksmith but not as muscular. Something seemed to be giving him extraordinary strength, though, as he pummeled the blacksmith.

Faith struggled to her feet and gave in to the urge to run. She fled, stumbling through the brush. She could see a clearing but twisted her ankle on a tree root and fell, sobbing. "It wasn't right," she repeated over and over. "It wasn't right."

Slade was soon at her side, shushing her. He helped her to her feet and held her as she cried a never-ending river of tears.

"I didn't want that to happen. I don't understand, but I-I felt so very frightened. Why would he do that? What did he want?"

"My little Boston bride," Slade murmured as he pressed his lips against her forehead and held her until she stopped trembling. "He's an animal. He probably thought you would feel compelled to marry him if he took your innocence."

"Oh…oh, oh my," Faith said, raising her hand to her cheek, truly understanding for the first time what had almost happened.

"Faith," Slade said, holding her at arm's length and giving her a shake. "I can no longer stand by and watch the men in this town circling you like a pack of hyenas moving in for the kill. You are going to marry me. Is that understood?"

Faith froze, at a loss for words. Slade, with his thumb, wiped the tears from her cheek until she found her voice.

She looked at Slade, really looked at him. His calm demeanor, his eyes, shining bright in the moonlight, drew her in like a magnet. She melted into him and whispered, "Yes, Slade, I will marry you." A feeling of peace and contentment such as she had never known before came over her. She lay her head against his shoulder and sighed with happiness.

"But, first, we have a matter to attend to." He scowled and took Faith to a tree stump hidden behind the brush. He pulled her to him, over his lap, and before she could get her bearings, he was applying the flat of his hand to her bottom, spanking her over and over again. "This is for running from me. You will never do that again. I am your safe harbor, Faith. From this moment on, you will always run toward me, never away."

He finished and righted her, seating her on his lap. Faith felt like a small child as she leaned her head into the crook of his neck, safe in the knowledge that she belonged to Slade and that he would forever take care of her.

Slade carried a disheveled Faith back through the fairgrounds, past the vendor booths and games and placed her gently in his surrey. Her twisted ankle was elevated and firmly wrapped by her concerned fiancé.

Slade didn't seem to like the idea of taking Faith back to the boarding house. "I want you home with me, where you belong. I have to warn you, Faith, I don't possess much patience. Once I've made up my mind, I take action. We will be married as soon as possible. Is that understood?"

"Yes, Slade. Whenever you say," Faith said, gifting him with her biggest smile. She knew she must look a sight with her hair loose and dress torn, but she didn't care. She knew she was pleasing in Slade's eyes, and that's all that mattered.

Slade carried Faith into the house, setting her carefully on the settee. Mrs. Reynolds, Mrs. Barnes, and Charity bustled around her, thanking Slade for bringing her safely home. After he left, the questions began.

"How did you get home before I did?" she asked, looking around, confused.

"I suspect you two took the scenic route home," Mrs. Reynolds said, her eyes twinkling.

"Faith, for goodness sakes, tell us what happened! We saw Mr. Miller carrying you through the fairgrounds," Mrs. Barnes urged.

"It was so romantic!" Charity added with a sigh.

"Everyone saw?" Faith asked, flustered.

"Oh, yes, dear, and let me tell you, it created quite a sensation. You two are the talk of the town," Mrs. Reynolds said, her eyes twinkling.

"Are you all right, dear?" Mrs. Barnes asked. "Don't tell anyone anything until I get back here with a cup of tea for you," the kindly woman added, bustling out of the room.

For the first time, Charity and Mrs. Reynolds noticed Faith's appearance, her swollen ankle and torn dress. Her hair was undone, with twigs and bits of brush in it.

Mrs. Reynolds and Charity pulled over a footstool to elevate her leg, and Mrs. Barnes was soon back with the tea. Faith gratefully took it from her and took a long sip. She took a look around as the women pulled chairs up to sit nearby. Charity sat at her feet, unwrapping her ankle and inspecting it.

"What happened, dear?" asked Mrs. Barnes.

"And don't leave out anything!" Mrs. Reynolds added.

"Well, I went to see the dancing and tried a few steps."

"Is that how you hurt your ankle?" Charity asked.

"No, that came later. Mr. Tikaani, the blacksmith, you know how he seemed to be around all the time?" Faith asked the women.

"Yes, and I told you to give that one a wide berth," Mrs. Reynolds said, her eyes narrowing. "Did he hurt you?" she asked.

"Yes, I mean, no," Faith began, flustered to have to speak out loud about what had happened.

"Go on, dear, tell us all about it," Mrs. Barnes said, patting Faith's hand.

"Well, he asked me to dance. He didn't really ask, though, he just sort of grabbed me."

All three women gasped, and Mrs. Reynolds began to fan herself as if she were about to swoon.

"I told him no. I pushed him away and left the dance floor. I began to walk back toward the vending area, but he followed. H-he, well, he p-pushed me into the brush and fell on top of me."

"Oh, no," Mrs. Barnes exclaimed.

"Did he press his advantage?" asked Mrs. Reynolds carefully.

Faith saw that Charity had tears in her eyes.

"Don't be upset, dear," Faith said, patting Charity's cheek. "He did have the advantage; he was so massive. I began to scream for help. Suddenly—" Here, she stopped, managing a small smile because she had such a rapt audience. "Suddenly, someone pulled him off of me. It was Slade. He pulled Mr. Tikaani to his feet and lit into him until the evil man ran off, bleeding from the mouth."

"So nothing bad happened?" Mrs. Reynolds asked.

"You weren't …" Charity began but was unable to go on.

"How far did he go, Faith? You must tell us," said Mrs. Barnes with great concern.

"No, nothing happened. Really," Faith assured the concerned women. "Slade got there in time."

"Thank God," said Mrs. Reynolds, leaning back in her chair.

"Slade?" Charity asked. Ever since Faith had come back from their business dinner, it had been "Slade," no more "Mr. Miller."

"Yes, Slade," Faith replied. "He said that he was tired of watching all the men in town fighting over me and that I was going to marry him, and that was that."

A squeal of excitement came from Charity. Mrs. Reynolds smiled knowingly, and Mrs. Barnes looked stunned.

"And how did you reply, dear?" Mrs. Barnes asked, afraid to rejoice just yet.

"I said yes, of course."

At that, all three women clapped and cheered.

"My, my, looks like you matched Mr. Miller up with the wrong sister," Mrs. Barnes chided Mrs. Reynolds.

"I was close, and I'm going to consider this to be one of my more successful matches."

"You go right ahead," said Faith, now grinning from ear to ear.

"Wonderful! Now, I only have to worry about one more bride," said Mrs. Reynolds, glaring at Charity.

Charity acted like Mrs. Reynolds was not, right this minute, giving her the evil eye. "But this business with the blacksmith. It needs to be reported to the sheriff," she pointed out.

"Yes, of course, but not tonight," said Faith, suddenly weary.

Everyone agreed that it had been a long night and sleep was desperately needed. Charity helped Faith up the stairs and put her to bed.

"I am just so glad you are all right, my sweet sister," said Charity, once she had brushed all the twigs out of her sister's hair and braided it. She got Faith tucked safely into bed.

"I'm fine, Charity. But how about you? How did you feel when you heard that Slade proposed to me? I need to know if it makes you feel at all bad, even just a little."

"Sister, at first glance, I could see that Mr. Miller was a fine man. And it was one of the hardest things I've ever done to tell him I'd changed my mind. But if we'd married, I don't think either one of us would have been content. I know I would never have felt the way you felt when you told us you'd accepted his proposal," she said with unwavering certainty. "Slade Miller will make a fine brother-in-law. It was all meant to unfold this way, I'm certain of it."

Charity bussed Faith on the forehead and made her exit. Faith lay there staring into the darkness, thinking things over. She, too, believed that it was all meant to be—the move to Wyoming, meeting Slade, their relationship growing of its own accord. She smiled and hugged herself, turning to her side and falling into a weary sleep.

All too soon, the sun was rising, and Faith, her ankle much better, went along with Charity and Mrs. Reynolds to tell her story to the sheriff. The sheriff did not seem surprised to hear what she had to say and shared some news with them.

"The blacksmith's house burned to the ground during the night. He and his horse are missing. After hearing what happened, I'm not surprised. I'm afraid it will be difficult, if not impossible, to track him down at this point. If he shows his face in these parts again, though, he'll be held accountable," he assured Faith.

Faith thanked the sheriff, glad that there wouldn't be a trial or a lynching. On their way back to the boarding house, Faith told the women, "At first, I felt responsible for having encouraged him by being nice whenever we met up. But as I was telling the sheriff what happened, I realized that Yuri Tikaani is a troubled man. I hope he returned to his family in Canada and never comes back."

"He won't come back," assured Charity.

"How do you know?" asked Faith, surprised.

"Because he's a coward; that's why," said Charity.

And Faith knew in her heart of hearts that what Charity said was true. The last she had seen of Yuri Tikaani was when he pulled away from Slade, bleeding from the mouth, looking terrified. Good riddance, she thought as she, Charity, and Mrs. Reynolds headed back to the boarding house.

CHAPTER 11

*F*all was coming. Faith could feel it, a subtle shift in the early morning temperature, a golden leaf swirling past, fog hanging heavy in the air. She hugged her shawl around her as she waited for the buggy that would take her to Hope's ranch. Faith was going to help with the cooking and baking for a big event happening at the ranch. She shivered with excitement as she thought about sharing the news of her engagement with Hope and Noble. Tonight, Slade would pick her up, and he planned to meet with Noble, the male head of the family, to ask for her hand.

Yes, the end of summer was rapidly approaching, and Mrs. Reynolds would soon board the train to return to Boston. The matchmaker was growing anxious that Charity was still single, declaring that none of the young ladies she'd ever kept at the boarding house with her had remained single for more than a few weeks. But then, Mrs. Reynolds had never met the likes of her little sister. Charity never spoke of any man in particular, and Faith wondered if she was still pining for the long-lost Thomas.

Faith adjusted the basket of bread she had hanging from her arm; she'd spent all yesterday baking two dozen loaves. Faith had told Pastor Gregory about her engagement to Slade, but he had already heard about the merchant carrying her through the fairgrounds. He had been disappointed but had taken it well, once Faith asked him to officiate at the wedding.

She reflected on Pastor Gregory's sermon last Sunday. He had spoken about having a servant's heart and a servant's hands. Faith liked that, the idea of finding spiritual fulfillment in the service of others.

Faith thought more about having a servant's heart and hands, the peace that came over her when she was baking for others. She had occasionally done so in Boston when her church fed the poor, but here in Wyoming, she'd had much more opportunity. She helped Mrs. Barnes with the baking for the boarders at the boarding house, she helped Slade and Nate at the store, occasionally, helping customers while the men put in supplies in the back, and she was pleased to have this opportunity to help Hope. There was nothing better than to be busy with one's hands, doing God's work, she reflected.

She was shaken from her reverie when Mr. Ender's buggy appeared through the mist and pulled up beside her. Instead of Noble driving, it was Bertha, the boyish farm foreman. Bertha extended a hand and helped Faith up into the wagon. Her eyes widened at the basket of bread Faith held on her lap.

"Hello there, I've been wanting to have a chat with you," Bertha said, giving Faith a sideways glance. Faith smiled at her shyly.

"Your sister is the best thing to happen on that ranch," Bertha declared with a western twang. "She is good with Noble and Gracie. Took right away to ranch life, she did. And what about you, Miss Faith? Have you taken to Wyoming?"

"I should hope so; I'm getting married in two weeks' time!" Faith shared. She was surprised at how easy Bertha was to talk to. "Hope is younger than I am, did you know that?" Faith asked.

"You don't say," Bertha said. "I just assumed she was the oldest."

"Everyone does," chuckled Faith. "She isn't by nature very domestic. I taught her everything she knows about baking."

"Well, you'd never know it. She has that ranch running like clockwork, she does," said Bertha, shaking her head in wonder.

"Hope has endless energy and a great outlook. Did she tell you that she wants to homestead and get her own land?" asked Faith.

"She did," declared Bertha.

"What do you think of that?" Faith asked.

"She's a smart lady, your sister. But she said she won't let any man work the land, only us womenfolk," added Bertha.

"Hope acts like she has something to prove," mused Faith.

"Maybe she does, maybe she does," said Bertha. "I'm glad you'll be helping with the cooking today. It's time to gather up the cattle for shipping. A busy time on the ranch, for sure," she stated, nodding her head sagely.

"And how did you come to be in Wyoming?" asked Faith. Bertha looked like she'd lived here all her life.

"Practically born and raised here," Bertha said with a snort of pride. "My parents were covered wagon folk, riding in from the east. I was born on the trail, right on the border of Wyoming, and my ma says I grew up wild. And I'm proud of it. I can ride and shoot and lasso as good as any man."

"Probably better than most," Faith agreed.

Soon, the wagon was driving under the "Triple E" wrought iron arch and into the ranch. Faith looked around in awe. The fog lay heavy, and she could just catch glimpses of the cowboys on horseback and hear the lowing sound the cattle made. They pulled up in front of the ranch house. Bertha helped Faith down and recommended that she hurry on in as Hope had been 'up and at 'em since before the sun came up'.

Faith entered the kitchen and took an apron off the wall. She looked around with wonder. She had never seen so much food in one place. Hope seemed to be preparing to feed an army of workers. Maria Tallfeather was standing at the stove, stirring a pot of beans and gave Faith a nod.

Hope came into the kitchen and ran over to give Faith a hug.

"You're here!" she exclaimed. "We have a lot of work to do, Faith. There will be an extra lot of farm hands here today. We need all the pies and biscuits you can produce. And thank you for this bread!" she added, lifting the cloth covering them to admire the loaves.

"Before we get started, Hope, there's something I want to tell you," Faith said, bursting with her news. "I'm engaged to be married."

Hope, who had already headed towards the oven, whirled around and stared, open-mouthed, at her sister. "Who's the lucky man?" she finally managed to ask.

"Mr. Slade Miller," Faith said, keeping a straight face. After a moment, both sisters burst into laughter.

"Good for you. Handsome man. Any woman would think him a good catch."

"Except our foolish little sister," agreed Faith.

"Is Charity all right with the news?" Hope asked.

"She seems excited about the whole thing."

"No regrets?"

"None that I've seen. I suspect she's still carrying a torch for Thomas."

"Have you seen any more of that young man we saw her talking to that day? The cowboy who looked like Thomas?"

"I have not and, believe me, I have kept an eye out for him. Charity, of course, has nothing to say on the subject. Say, who is coming here to help today?" Faith asked, looking again at the food sitting on the sideboard.

"The other ranchers and their ranch hands. It's a traveling thing, with each of the ranchers taking turns helping each other with the shipping at this time of year."

Faith set herself at the baking station, and there she stood all day, turning out big tins of biscuits and at least two dozen pies. Time passed quickly, and before she knew it, she and Hope were cleaning up. Noble came in and gave his wife a kiss. He announced that he would saddle up the horses to take Faith home.

"You don't have to, Mr. Enders. There's a gentleman who is coming to get me. He has something to discuss with you, if you're not too tired."

"Who is this?" Noble asked, "and what does he have to say for himself?"

"It's Mr. Miller from the mercantile and, well, he wants to marry me."

"He's coming to ask my blessing? That's right and proper." Noble nodded. "Although, he should have done this before asking you."

"Well, something happened, and I think it's time I told you two about it," Faith said. She knew everyone must be exhausted, but instead, Hope and Noble were suddenly wide awake. Little Grace had been put to bed, and they had the main room to themselves.

Faith slowly began to tell her story, complete with Mr. Tikaani's dastardly behavior at the county fair, how her savior, Slade, had come to the rescue, and the unique way in which he had proposed, leaving out the part about the spanking.

"The next time I see that blacksmith…" Noble began, flexing his jaw.

"He left that night after burning his house to the ground. No one has seen him since."

"If he knows what's good for him, he'll stay away," Hope added, looking as fiercely protective as her husband.

Faith had managed to get through the story without losing her composure, but now the tears began to fall. It was the first time she'd had to relive the nightmare since she'd informed the sheriff about the attack. Hope and Noble gathered around her and patted her arms, reassuring her that she was safe now.

"I know that," said Faith, smiling reassuringly at them.

"And Slade Miller, you've taken a shine to him?" Noble asked.

"I've spent a lot of time with Slade, selling my pies at the mercantile, even helping behind the counter at times. I've come to care for him very deeply, much more so than any of the men Mrs. Reynolds was trying to match me with."

"Well, that's good, then," said Hope.

Noble had gone to look out of the front window of the ranch house. Suddenly, he pointed and said, "There he is."

Faith stood, but Hope held her back. Noble went out to the front porch, closing the door behind him. The men stayed outside for some time until the sky began to darken. Occasionally, Faith would peek through the window and see the glow of their lit cigars as they talked together. She could hear voices, but she could not make out what they were saying.

"Whatever are they discussing?" Faith wondered aloud, pacing back and forth.

"Your future," said Hope. "Noble will want to make sure that you'll be properly taken care of. Does Slade want children?" Hope asked.

"His children are grown, a son and a daughter. He has a three-year-old grandson, by his daughter. He said he doesn't care whether we have children or not."

"Being that he's in a different place in life, I guess that's true," said Hope. "And when will the marriage take place?" She steered Faith towards the kitchen and poured a couple cups of tea. "Come on, sister. Have a seat."

"Slade says he's a man of action and that we'll marry as soon as it can be put together. That should be in another week or so," Faith replied, sitting down at the table.

"Are you prepared for the demands of marriage, Faith?" asked Hope, sitting in the chair next to her eldest sister.

"I'm perfectly capable of running a household, as you well know," Faith retorted.

"I don't mean those demands. I mean the demands of the marriage bed," Hope said patiently.

Faith put her hand to her face as her cheeks pinkened. "For Heaven's sake, Hope, I'm not going to discuss this with my younger sister."

"Who, then?" asked Hope.

"I dare say no one had this discussion with any of the brides on the bride train," Faith protested.

"How would you know?" asked Hope. "Faith, sex can be a somewhat…messy…proposition. And there's more to sex than just the man mounting the woman. How much do you know?"

"I think I have an idea of what happens between a man and a woman, Hope," protested Faith. She could not wait for this conversation to end.

"Slade is not a boy, Faith. He is a grown man, and he may want to do more than make love in the missionary position."

"What more?" Faith asked, suddenly unsure.

"Married couples use various bodily openings to bring pleasure to each other. You'll have to learn what he likes."

"Various…" Faith began but then stopped and stared at Hope. "I have no idea what you are talking about," she scolded. "And I suspect you don't, either."

Hope laughed at this. "Just relax, at first, Faith. Let whatever happens happen. Keep an open mind. Don't be shocked by what he may eventually ask of you. It's all perfectly normal," she replied, patting Faith's hand. "And if you have any questions later, I'm here to help."

Just then the door opened, and the two men walked in. Faith's eyes lit up as she took in her fiancé's face. She ran up and gave him a kiss in greeting. Slade was smiling, and Noble looked content. Faith realized the talk must have gone well.

"Come into the kitchen, gentlemen; I managed to hide away a small pie today," she said. "Let's have coffee and pie."

"How did you manage that?" Hope asked. Everything that wasn't nailed down seemed to have disappeared quickly as the hungry cowboys had devoured everything set before them.

"While you ladies brew up the coffee, Noble can help me bring in the supplies," said Slade.

"Supplies?" Hope and Noble asked in unison.

"Of course, I can't show up at my future in-laws' empty handed."

Slade smiled. "I figured, after today, you folks would need flour, sugar, corn meal, you know, staples."

"Well, we certainly do, and that's mighty kind of you," said Noble.

"Mighty kind," agreed Hope.

Slade had brought a great deal more than a few staples. After the bounty had all been put away, the two couples sat around the table, eating and talking. Slade and Noble spoke about the shipping season and the rhythm and flow of life on a cattle ranch. They talked for quite some time as Faith took it all in—her husband-to-be, her sister's husband, Hope, and herself—the two couples sitting together, forging family bonds over pie and coffee.

Suddenly, Hope looked up and out the window.

"It's pitch black outside, tonight, hardly any moonlight, plus, a wind has started up."

"You will stay here and depart in the morning," Noble announced, and Slade agreed.

It was decided that Faith would sleep with Grace and Slade was shown to the guest room.

Faith slipped into a too large nighty that Hope had supplied and slid into a feather bed next to her sleeping niece. She had just dozed off when she was awoken by a sound. She lay in the darkness trying to figure out what it was. A loose shutter hitting the side of the house? Branches hitting the window? But it seemed to be coming from inside.

She slipped out of bed and tiptoed down the darkened hallway, looking for the source of the sound. She came upon a room with the door ajar, light spilling out into the hallway. The sound was coming from inside the room. She tiptoed to the doorway and peeked inside. She saw Noble, with her sister, Hope, lying over his lap. Her sister's bottom was bared and pinkened, her feet stretched out behind her, toes gripping the floor.

Noble was holding the wooden paddle they kept on their bedroom wall. He was speaking softly but firmly to his wife, scolding her for some transgression. Hope was pleading with him, and Faith could make out enough to know that she was afraid their guests would overhear her disciplinary session.

This didn't seem to sway Noble, and he again began to paddle away, her sister's buttocks jumping and jiggling as the board made contact. Faith felt a clenching between her legs as she stared at the strangely stimulating scene before her.

Suddenly, a hand covered her mouth as she was pulled back against a rock-hard body.

"Shhh," someone whispered in her ear, and she realized it was Slade. He had come up behind her and had caught her in the act of peeking at Hope and Noble during a most private moment.

"You naughty girl," he whispered in her ear. "Spying on your sister's disciplinary session. Why, I do believe you have earned a spanking of your own."

Again, Faith felt that clenching between her legs, and she almost swooned. It was only Slade's arm around her rib cage, under her breasts, that kept her on her feet. He let go of her and held out his hand. Sheepishly, Faith took it and followed her fiancé back down the hallway to his room.

She stood here, flushed, waiting to explain herself. Slade shut the door firmly and then sat on the bed.

"Slade, I was just…I heard a noise. I went to investigate."

But he did not seem to care to hear what she had to say. "Did you stay and watch? Tell me the truth," he whispered.

Faith hung her head, embarrassed. She had indeed stayed longer than she needed to.

"Come, Faith," he said, patting his lap.

Faith could hardly believe this was happening. Awkwardly, she moved to her fiancé's side.

"Right on over. You know you deserve this," he scolded.

Faith fought the urge to turn and run. Instead, she awkwardly climbed over her fiancé's lap until her tummy was on his thighs. She tensed as he began to lift the hem of her nightgown. He wouldn't completely undress her, would he? She squirmed as the back of her gown was pushed up to her waist, shocked when Slade began to undo the sides of her drawers.

"No, please," she moaned softly, as afraid as Hope had been that someone would overhear.

Soon, she could feel the cool air on the skin of her bottom. There were no illusions as to what her fiancé could see. She'd just seen the same view of her sister.

As Slade began to spank, she murmured and moved, surprised at how much a man's hand could hurt. He didn't speak, just spanked away until she was crying tears of remorse.

Finally, he allowed her to rise, held her as she sat on his lap, sobbing.

"What kind of a husband would I be if I didn't correct my little wife when she needed it?" he whispered, bussing her on the forehead.

"Yes, sir," Faith replied, realizing that Slade would be her true spiritual leader—the only husband she could ever accept.

CHAPTER 12

*F*aith was bustling between the vanity in the room Slade had set aside for her to get ready in and the dining room. She kept checking the food. She was wearing her best blue silk and had pinned an apron across the front. She stopped for a moment, lost in thought, wondering how much they would entertain in the years to come.

She hurried back to the vanity. Although she was dressed, her hair wouldn't cooperate. She planned to wear it swept up atop her head, but it was so fine that, as usual, it was tumbling about her shoulders. Just as she was about to give up, in the looking glass, she saw Charity enter the room behind her.

"Here, let me do that," her little sister said. Faith breathed a sigh of relief. Charity always could work magic with her hair. Soon, she was deftly twisting the strands and pinning it atop her head.

"And these loose ends, Charity, make sure you gather those up, too."

"No, sister, let the curls around your neck and the sides of your face fall free. They soften your appearance. Why are you wearing your blue silk, Faith? I'm sure Mr. Miller would have bought you a proper wedding gown."

"Not until we're married," said Faith. "I'll not take anything from him until then, and my blue silk is fine."

"Stand up now and let me see you," said Charity. "Why, Faith, you've never looked prettier!"

Faith ducked and turned, looking at her reflection in the looking glass. Her cheeks were pink and her eyes shone with excitement.

"Well, I should hope so," she declared. "It's my wedding day!"

"And tonight, is your wedding night," added Hope, entering the room.

Faith gave Hope a hug and then rushed back out to the kitchen to check her pies. She was keeping them warm in the warming drawer.

Just then, Mrs. Barnes entered the kitchen, carrying a cake. "I know you are serving pie for dessert tonight, dear, but a bridal couple should have a wedding cake."

"Oh, Mrs. Barnes, you shouldn't have gone to so much trouble," Faith cried. But the cake was lovely, and she watched, fascinated, as Mrs. Barnes set it on the sideboard and carefully set a china figurine of two love birds on top. She then took some flowers out of her basket and arranged them around the cake.

"It's lovely," Charity agreed. Mrs. Reynolds followed behind and set a wrapped gift on a side table.

Faith was too busy to see it; she was bustling between the kitchen and dining room bringing out more food.

"I thought it was just us, Faith," said Charity. "There's enough food here for a community dinner."

"There will be a few others," said Faith. "And I won't have it said that the new Mrs. Miller doesn't know how to entertain."

Just then, Noble arrived with Grace in tow, and Nate followed them, climbing the stairs from the shop.

"All closed up for the day!" he explained. "It's mighty nice of you folks to include me."

"Of course!" said Faith. She took Grace aside and asked her to be her flower girl.

The little girl nodded, looking serious. "What does a flower girl do?" she asked, ready to meet her responsibilities.

Charity took over, explaining about walking ahead of the bride and dropping flowers. She handed Grace the little basket that Faith had adorned with ribbons and filled with flower petals.

Faith and Slade had planned a candlelight ceremony. As the candles were lit, the room took on a warm glow. Faith couldn't wait for Slade to see it. Her groom was downstairs getting ready, because Mrs. Reynolds believed it was bad luck for the wedding couple to see each other the day of the wedding.

The last to arrive was Pastor Gregory, looking distinguished in his pastoral apparel. Faith smiled warmly at him, and he let her know, with an equally warm smile in return, that he had made peace with this marriage and was ready to bless the union.

Mrs. Reynolds sat down at the spinet piano and began to play scales. Hope came to stand beside Faith.

"Being able to play the wedding march is a good skill for a matchmaker to have," she observed.

"That's for certain," little Grace piped up, stepping in between them.

There was a knock on the door, and Faith froze in place.

"What is it?" Charity asked.

"What's wrong?" asked Hope.

"It must be Slade's children; they were due to arrive on the six o'clock."

"That's right," said Charity. "He has a grown son and daughter, isn't that right?"

"And a son-in-law, and a little grandson," added Faith growing pale with nerves.

Charity stood next to Faith and rubbed her arm. "I'm sure they'll love you."

"Don't expect much," said Hope under her breath. "Don't come on strong; let them find their way to you when they're ready."

Charity and Hope pulled Faith back into her room as Nate greeted the callers and took them downstairs to see their father.

Faith remembered something and ran into the kitchen, her sisters following. She pulled a pan of streusel out of the warming tray.

"Streusel?" Hope asked, one eyebrow raised.

"Mother's recipe. I thought it was fitting, because Slade is half German, as are we.

"You sure you don't want to put that away for breakfast?" asked Charity. Faith shook her head no as Charity went on, "I'm sure you'll love living close to Mrs. Barnes and the boarding house. You'll be able to keep her in pies."

"What are you talking about?" Hope scolded. "Faith is going to have her hands full between helping out at the mercantile and keeping house."

"Oh, I'll still be baking, and it won't take any extra time at all to send a couple of pies over to the boarding house."

"See!" said Charity, smiling smugly.

They could hear Mrs. Reynolds beginning to play the prelude to the Wedding March in earnest.

Mrs. Barnes poked her head into the room. "It's almost time."

"Are you excited?" Faith asked Grace, who couldn't stop hopping up and down.

"Yes, ma'am," she said with a giggle.

"Grace, I'm your aunt, you know. You can call me Aunt Faith. And I want to start teaching you how to bake. Would you come stay with me sometime and help me make pies?"

Grace smiled shyly and nodded.

"At the age of eight, I was already baking cookies and even cakes. I want you to learn how, too."

"Thankee, Auntie," said Grace.

Faith made a mental note to work on Grace's speech. The child might have grown up running wild on the ranch, but she was going to end up as a refined young lady, if Faith had anything to say about it. They both looked up sharply as a child's cry was heard coming from the other room.

"Are there other children here?" Grace asked.

"It's little Sam, your Uncle Slade's grandson. He's three, as I recall."

"Oh, goodie!" Grace exclaimed. "A cousin!"

"Yes, Grace, you'll be his cousin," said Charity, and they laughed as the little girl's eyes grew wide. Faith realized that by saying "I do," she was forming family ties. Soon, she would have a stepson and stepdaughter, a son-in-law, and a grandson.

Faith went to the door and listened. She could just make out Slade's voice. He was in place as the prelude to the Wedding March ended. Faith stood and prepared to join him at the appointed place. Hope and Charity stopped her from opening the door. Charity gave her hair a few last touches as Hope removed her apron.

"Goodness, now I know why brides have bridesmaids," Faith said, laughing. "Else I might have gotten married in my pinnings."

Charity embraced her sister, tears in her eyes, and kissed her on the cheek. Hope handed Faith a small Bible wrapped in soft white leather. It was bedecked with ribbons and a flower on top.

"A gift from Charity and myself to carry on your trip to the altar," she said, smiling.

"Thank you." Faith beamed. "I don't know what I'd do without you, either of you." She swallowed hard and blinked her eyes, afraid to start crying before she even started down the aisle. Hope and Charity moved in close around her, and the three sisters held hands, Hope leading a prayer.

"Dear Heavenly Father, please bless our sister, Faith, as she begins the walk toward her destiny, Slade Miller."

Charity squeezed Faith's hand and added, "I'm so proud of you, sister. Look what a journey you've taken, from the kitchen in our little brownstone to Slade Miller's arms."

Mrs. Reynolds played louder as she launched into The Wedding March. Little Grace was peeking out of the bedroom door and turned to announce, "It's time. Let's go."

Hope and Charity slipped out of the door and took their seats. Grace opened the door and walked down between the chairs to where Slade was standing. Then, Faith exited the room and began to walk toward her fiancé, overwhelmed at the thought that, within moments, he would be her husband. At that moment, she realized how little she knew him, but a smile spread over her face and she forgot her nerves as she reveled in the knowledge that they had the rest of their lives to learn about one another.

Faith said a little prayer of her own as she walked toward him, holding her bridal Bible. *Dear God, please bless this union; please let me be pleasing in his sight.* She had always secretly wondered if she was the consolation prize—a not-quite-as-good replacement for Charity, but the look in Slade's eyes at that moment made her realize that he truly loved her. He was as moved by this moment as she, and her heart swelled with a happiness she'd never known before.

She was hardly aware of anyone else in the room, only having eyes for the man at her side. They said their vows, each to the other, and when the minister pronounced them husband and wife, Slade took her in his arms for a masterful kiss. At that moment, something within her melted, a core of suffering, the hardship of her childhood, the fear that had kept her from truly experiencing life. It was all swept away when her new husband kissed her, sealing their bond with the promise of spending the rest of their lives together. Faith made a silent vow to be the best wife that she could be.

Afterward, the wedding guests surrounded them, the women wishing the bride well, the men congratulating the bridegroom. Faith was introduced to her step-children and grandchild. Slade's son, Evan, looked just like him, tan with swept back brown hair. His face was open as he greeted his new step-mother warmly.

Slade's daughter must resemble her mother, Faith thought. She was small, dark, and pretty, smiling but with a guarded look in her eye. Little Sam was a blond angel, even though he was tired and fussy. Grace stepped up and took over with the little lad, clearly smitten with her new cousin.

Nate and Pastor Gregory both kissed the bride. A fiddle was produced, the chairs moved back, and the rug rolled up, then spontaneous dancing broke out. While Faith danced a waltz with her new husband, Hope, Mrs. Barnes, and Mrs. Reynolds uncovered the food and began to urge people to eat.

As she sat next to her husband eating their bridal dinner, Faith looked at each of her guests. Nate was chatting with Mrs. Barnes; Slade was laughing with his children. Charity appeared to be suffering through a lecture by Mrs. Reynolds, probably about her single status. This was Jeanette's final night in Wyoming. Tomorrow, she would leave by rail for Boston. Faith realized that she did not envy Mrs. Reynolds, not with one fiber of her being. Overcast and gloomy Boston seemed very far away. She would not want to see the last of sunny Wyoming. By taking a husband, she had committed herself to this new land. She and her sisters would build families and grow old right here in Wyoming, and the prospect filled her with unadulterated happiness.

She looked over at her husband and covered his hand with hers, smiling into his warm blue eyes. Together, they would manage the farm and run the store. She looked forward to a future she could not even have imagined, sitting in her little kitchen in Boston.

Later, after their guests had trickled away, Faith and Slade sat together, staring into the fireplace.

"You know, some believe that you can see your future in the flames," said Slade.

Faith looked at him searchingly and then realized by the crinkles in the corner of his eyes that he was hiding a smile. She decided to play along. She lay her head on his shoulder and asked, "What do you see?"

"I see a store that will grow to encompass the third floor, a beautiful new house, travel and contributing to our growing community. Perhaps we'll sit on the board of that new opera house Charity can't stop talking about."

Faith's head swam at the visions Slade was invoking with his words. "A house?" she asked. "Can we afford that, along with the store and the farm?"

"That and much, much more," Slade informed her, amused that his little bride had married him without seeming to have any idea of his net worth. He handed her a package that was sitting on the settee next to him.

"What is this?" Faith asked, puzzled.

"A gift from Mrs. Reynolds. She told me that you were to open it tonight, before we go to bed."

Faith opened the box and removed a flimsy pink garment. With a blush, she realized it was a piece of lingerie, a gown.

"I do believe I'd like to see you in that," Slade said, nuzzling her neck.

Faith gasped and gathered the gown to her, running towards the room she'd gotten ready in, aghast that Slade had even seen such a garment. She held it up in front of the mirror, studying her reflection. She understood that one should wear a garment of this nature on the wedding night, but it didn't appear to be very warm or practical.

Her wedding night! Faith paused for a moment and looked around the room, one of four bedrooms on the third floor. It was furnished as nicely as the others, with high-end items shipped from back east. Her wedding night would not be spent in a log cabin, nor would it happen in a Boston townhouse or a rustic ranch somewhere. Instead, it would happen here, in these lavish quarters above the mercantile. She washed from the wash basin then donned the garment. She had never felt anything quite like it against her skin. It positively slithered down her body. Faith took down her hair and brushed it out. Finally, she felt ready for her wedding night.

She donned a dressing gown and stepped outside of the room to find her new husband sitting in the parlor, watching the dying embers flickering in the fireplace. When he heard her, he stood and turned to face her, looking handsome in his night shirt and dressing gown. She had relished the look on his face as she'd walked down the aisle, but it did not come close to the look of adoration he had now. She went into his arms.

"Did you enjoy your wedding?" he murmured into her ear.

Faith pulled back and looked up at her spouse. "Very much. It was perfect," she announced.

He pulled her to him again, and she buried her nose in the lapel of his dressing gown, suddenly feeling shy and awkward. He smelled of soap and sandalwood, amber and spices, and something else, a hint of peppermint. Faith longed to melt into the very core of him, surprised at the emotions that her husband holding her were eliciting.

Slade took her by the hand and led her to his bedroom, a room that had a small fireplace glittering against the far wall. He had brought some of the candles from the living room into his private quarters. The bed was large and ornate, a man's bed. He turned to Faith and covered her face with soft, sweet kisses, which took her breath away. As his kisses traveled down her neck, her growing arousal emboldened her to pull him tight against her, running her hands along the expanse of his back.

"Open your eyes," Slade instructed her, his breath ragged.

Faith felt herself shudder. She had been nervous about this night, truth be told. She knew she had a duty to perform, but she had not counted on this, the flush, the tingling, the way her senses came alive and how it triggered her emotions.

The sensations his sensual touch ignited was nothing like anything she had experienced before. Slowly, Slade loosened her dressing gown and pushed it away from her shoulders. Faith stood frozen in place as he bent to pull back the coverlet to the bed. At Slade's urging, she lay on the bed, still in her night shift. She began to tremble with nerves, willing herself to stop. But instead of climbing in beside her, Slade went around the room extinguishing the candles until the room was dark.

She heard a rustling of clothes and then felt Slade climb into bed beside her. Instantly, she realized he was naked. Again, he began to rain kisses upon her, first, her forehead then moving his lips down to hers. He ran his hands down her neck until he had reached her gown, undoing the fastenings and pushing it away from her. Faith had calmed as her eyes had grown accustomed to the darkness, and she was able to see her dear husband's face. His eyes were heavy lidded, his breath growing ragged. Wantonly, she pulled him to her, gasping at the sensation of feeling his skin against hers. *Dear God, let me be as pleasing to him as he is to me. Let me never tire of holding him in my arms like this.*

She felt his lips trailing down her neck and to her chest, his kisses and gentle tugging at her breasts causing her to whimper and move against him. As he climbed atop her, for one wild moment, she wanted him to stop, but then his kisses resumed. As his hands worked their magic, she again became lost in the sensations. Suddenly, there was a sharp pain, over as quickly as it had begun.

He was inside of her, delving carefully, and then with increasing speed and force. Faith felt a primal urge and wrapped her legs around him, pulling him more deeply within. She didn't even realize she was crying, until she felt the moisture on Slade's own dear cheek.

"Am I hurting you?" he whispered.

She reveled in his breath upon her ear and his heart beating against hers. "For a moment, but not now. Don't stop," Faith moaned, and then her voice rose to a cry as she felt a warmth burst within her. She could not think, only feel, as her husband drove into her over and over until he stiffened and cried out her name then collapsed atop her.

Afterward, Faith lay in his arms, her head under his chin, her hand on her dear husband's abdomen.

"I love you," she said simply.

"And I love you, too," Slade responded.

As she lay there, listening to her husband's breathing slow and soften as he fell asleep, Faith thought about the journey that had brought her here, to this place. She had set out to enter an arranged marriage but, instead, had found love and a future she could never have envisioned sitting in the kitchen of her little townhouse in Boston. *Yes*, she decided, just as sleep was overtaking her, *moving to Wyoming had been the best choice the Cummings girls could ever have made.*

The End

WATCH for the two remaining books in the *"Three Cowboys for Three Sisters"* series:

A Haven of Hope, coming out in 2019 and

An Act of Charity, due in 2020.

VICTORIA WINTERS

Victoria Winters lives where the days are short and the nights run long. She loves the sight of bats flying in front of a full moon and the sound of waves crashing against rocks.

When not putting pen to paper, she serves as a Past Life Regressionist and seeker of Spiritual Truth in an eternal quest to merge the past with the future.

Victoria very much believes that everyone deserves to live happily ever after.

Don't miss these exciting titles by Victoria Winters and Blushing Books!

CPSIA information can be obtained
at www.ICGtesting.com
Printed in the USA
LVHW031315070921
697192LV00003B/491

9 781645 630388